©Noboru Kannatuki
MW00575814
15
GOBLIN SLAYER

"Drive like the wind, Master Lizard!"

She was like a blue gale,
a streak of cerulean light
tearing across the green
of the field.
©Noboru Kannatuki

Contents

GOBLIN SLAYER

VOLUME 15

KUMO KAGYU

Illustration by
NOBORU KANNATUKI

GOBLIN SLAYER

KUMO KAGYU

Translation by Kevin Steinbach ✣ Cover art by Noboru Kannatuki

Yen On
150 West 30th Street, 19th Floor
New York, NY 10001

Visit us at yenpress.com ✣ facebook.com/yenpress ✣ twitter.com/yenpress
yenpress.tumblr.com ✣ instagram.com/yenpress

First Yen On Edition: January 2023
Edited by Yen On Editorial: Rachel Mimms
Designed by Yen Press Design: Wendy Chan

Yen On is an imprint of Yen Press, LLC.
The Yen On name and logo are trademarks of Yen Press, LLC.

The publisher is not responsible for websites (or their content) that are not owned by the publisher.

Library of Congress Cataloging-in-Publication Data
Names: Kagyū, Kumo, author. | Kannatuki, Noboru, illustrator.
Title: Goblin slayer / Kumo Kagyu ; illustration by Noboru Kannatuki.
Other titles: Goburin sureiyā. English
Description: New York, NY : Yen On, 2016—
Identifiers: LCCN 2016033529 | ISBN 9780316501590 (v. 1 : pbk.) | ISBN 9780316553223 (v. 2 : pbk.) | ISBN 9780316553230 (v. 3 : pbk.) | ISBN 9780316411882 (v. 4 : pbk.) | ISBN 9781975326487 (v. 5 : pbk.) | ISBN 9781975327842 (v. 6 : pbk.) | ISBN 9781975330781 (v. 7 : pbk.) | ISBN 9781975331788 (v. 8 : pbk.) | ISBN 9781975331801 (v. 9 : pbk.) | ISBN 9781975314033 (v. 10 : pbk.) | ISBN 9781975322526 (v. 11 : pbk.) | ISBN 9781975325022 (v. 12 : pbk.) | ISBN 9781975333492 (v. 13 : pbk.) | ISBN 9781975345594 (v. 14 : pbk.) | ISBN 9781975350161 (v. 15 : pbk.)
Subjects: LCSH: Goblins—Fiction. | GSAFD: Fantasy fiction.
Classification: LCC PL872.5.A367 G6313 2016 | DDC 895.63/6—dc23
LC record available at https://lccn.loc.gov/2016033529

ISBNs: 978-1-9753-5016-1 (paperback)
978-1-9753-5017-8 (ebook)

10 9 8 7 6 5 4 3 2 1

LSC-C

Printed in the United States of America

GOBLIN SLAYER

VOLUME 15

"I am to goblins what goblins are to us."

GOBLIN SLAYER

A strange adventurer active on the frontier. He is famous for reaching Silver (3rd) rank hunting only goblins.

"Protect, heal, save."
—The Three Holy Tenets of the Earth Mother

PRIESTESS

Works with Goblin Slayer. A sweet young woman who must put up with her partner's antics.

"Ignorance is bliss, for learning is the highest joy." —Elven proverb

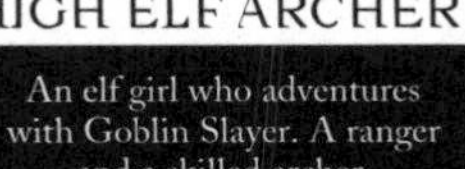

HIGH ELF ARCHER

An elf girl who adventures with Goblin Slayer. A ranger and a skilled archer.

The only things that matter to her are the weather, the animals, the crops…and him.

COW GIRL

A girl who works on the farm where Goblin Slayer lives. The two are old friends.

"How can you go adventuring without pen and paper?"

GUILD GIRL

A girl who works at the Adventurers Guild. Goblin Slayer's preference for goblin slaying always helps her out.

"Before they're polished, jewels and precious metals all look like rocks. No dwarf would judge a thing by its appearance alone."

DWARF SHAMAN

A dwarf spell caster who adventures with Goblin Slayer.

"A naga does not run."

LIZARD PRIEST

A lizardman priest who adventures with Goblin Slayer.

"Train yourself: Kill with the blade. If blood flows, let it be the enemy's."— First of the "Secrets of Steel."

HEAVY WARRIOR

A Silver-ranked adventurer associated with the Guild in the frontier town. Along with Female Knight and his other companions, his party is one of the best on the frontier.

"Only a tangled skein awaits those who carelessly spin tales about love or the universe's mysteries...not to mention a woman's beauty."

WITCH

A Silver-ranked adventurer at the frontier town's Adventurers Guild.

"I won't make friends tomorrow with an enemy I respect. I'll do it today."

SPEARMAN

A Silver-ranked adventurer at the frontier town's Adventurers Guild.

"Love does not consist in gazing at each other, but in looking outward in the same direction." —A poet

SWORD MAIDEN

Archbishop of the Supreme God in the water town. Also a Gold-ranked adventurer who once fought with the Demon Lord.

Too late to wage battle,
the enemy already lies far beyond.
But fall to your knees?
Kneeling would you never live.

Run, run, silver star!
The best, the worst:
You leave all behind.

Horses, horses, O fine horses!
The Valkyrie's blessing is for you alone.

Run, run, silver star!
The best, the worst:
You leave all behind.

CHAPTER 1

Rescue the Princess!

The first town gate she ever saw was so much bigger than she'd imagined.

It was so tall that she had to crane her neck to look up at it, which she did for a long moment before steeling herself and taking a step forward.

She walked resolutely, her footsteps clacking on the hard, tightly packed stones. Was it the gallant footsteps or the Dai Katana and greatbow the girl carried on her back, practically dwarfing her? Something made passersby look at her with interest, their gazes sharp enough to pierce. But when it came to piercing gazes, the girl's was as sharp as anyone's. It caused the interested onlookers to glance away, uneasy, and that was enough; the girl ignored them and walked on.

She was practically in enemy territory here. Everyone was on guard; no quarter would be afforded to her. And if she let her own vigilance slip, even for a second, this pack of wolves would be on her; they would tear her apart.

At least, so the girl believed. In her mind, there was no room for doubt.

Still... Still, the place was enough to make her dizzy. The road was stone. The buildings were stone. The sky seemed narrow and cramped, far away above the towering buildings. It was extraordinarily unsettling not to be able to see the horizon. The breeze was fetid, and the body heat from the crowd was overwhelming. Her ears were assaulted by a cacophony of sounds; it was chaotic, nary a blank space anywhere. A person could go mad in a place like this.

The girl shook her head and picked up her pace, as if she knew she would regret coming to a halt even accidentally. Her destination—everything was all right. She knew where she was going. At least…she was pretty sure she did. She'd imagined she would find it right away, but this town of stone was starting to sap her confidence. She couldn't show weakness, though. Her lip stiffened.

She worked her way through what seemed like a labyrinth to her. No weakness. No weakness. She couldn't look like a mark.

Thankfully, it didn't take as long as she'd feared to find her destination, and she made it there before twilight. That was due in part to the fact that all the streets had names, and there were plenty of signs saying which was which. Did that mean this was a trap? Or that even the people who lived here couldn't remember them all?

Well, even if it was a trap, there was nothing to do but spring it. The girl stood in front of the building she'd been looking for, a tavern with a sign shaped like an ax, and took a piece of paper out of her pouch: a letter, creased and worn from being opened and refolded so many times.

The girl studied the characters intently, looking back and forth between the paper and the sign to make sure she had it right. She did. This was the place.

There was a pair of saloon doors at about chest high, swaying gently open and shut. They hardly looked big enough to serve as doors. From the entrance came sound, light, noise, and an aroma of herbs and spices she had never smelled before. The girl, her senses overwhelmed, started to think she might not have the courage to take that next step.

But she couldn't let herself be beaten now. That was exactly what her enemies wanted.

The girl clenched her fist, got a good running start, and went charging into the maelstrom.

The hinge cried out at her assault, attracting another round of stares from those within, but the girl responded with her own look like a honed blade, sweeping away the too-interested gazes. At the same time, she looked around the tavern—and then, finally, her tense face bloomed like a flower.

She's as beautiful as ever!

With her lush hair tied easily on her head, it was as if the boisterous atmosphere didn't touch her beauty. Her figure was robust and yet womanly, showing how pathetic the girl's own spindly body was. She had her hair tied up the same way, in imitation of the older woman, but she couldn't help thinking that there was no comparing the two of them.

What should she say? Should she call out to the woman? Her mind ran in circles—but she mustn't panic. She forced down the impulse to shout and run over to the woman, instead taking a serious, careful step forward. It gave her the time to, somehow, wipe the smile off her face as she walked along in time to the creaking of the floorboards.

The other woman hadn't noticed her yet. Perfect.

Her relief was short-lived, however. The other woman was wearing—unbelievably—what appeared to be the outfit of a menial laborer.

The girl was somehow able to fend off the rush of blood to her head—but that, too, was only for a moment, until she saw the way the drunkard at the table reached for the woman, altogether too friendly. When the girl saw the woman try to push the man's hand away, disgusted, she finally lost control.

She dashed forward so hard that it seemed she would leave footprints in the wooden floor, and she reached for the katana on her back.

The man caught sight of her just before she drew her sword. She didn't care. How could she care?

"Get away from my sister!"

Whoosh! The sword sliced past the man's nose and grazed the tabletop. She'd been trying to cut off his arm, but the man had already moved out of the way.

What inexperience! Tears of rage and humiliation beaded in her eyes, but still the girl howled, "Where did you take the princess, you bastard?!"

"Huh?"

"Wha—?"

Heavy Warrior and Centaur Waitress looked at each other, both utterly confused.

§

"...I'm really not much for urban adventuring."

"I see." The bluntest possible answer. Goblin Slayer's grimy metal helmet shook from side to side.

The Adventurers Guild was filled with a pleasant burble that was, effectively, peace. In the waiting area, adventurers clad in and carrying every imaginable kind of equipment sat on the benches or otherwise congregated. Every single one of them seemed to be staring at Heavy Warrior, who was looking weak and out of sorts. Virtually no one outside his party had ever witnessed him this way, for the only times he'd acted anything like this were perhaps on his very first adventure—when he'd smacked his huge sword directly into a wall—and when he'd been sweating a promotion.

It was clear that the cause of his distress on this occasion was Female Knight, who was standing behind him and looking royally angry. Or did it have to do with the two centaur women standing some distance away? The smaller one was glaring around intimidatingly, trying to protect her rather confused older sister.

The young centaur girl had her black hair tied up and carried a huge katana and a giant bow across her back. Her hands and all four of her legs were armored in leather—lightly, by human standards.

"It looks a bit like the sort of equipment an elf would wear," observed Priestess with some admiration.

"I believe those are the weapons and armor of the people of the plain," Lizard Priest said, shaking his head on its long neck.

Not long ago, the young cleric might have been in a tizzy about this, but now she was unfazed.

Heavy Warrior cast a resentful gaze at Goblin Slayer. The malign influence he was having on this purehearted young girl!

"I don't know the circumstances," Goblin Slayer said.

"Well, neither do I!" Heavy Warrior insisted. He sighed, clearly at the end of his rope. If he didn't know what was going on, then of course Goblin Slayer wouldn't.

The grimy adventurer and the adventurer whose weapons had been taken from him: One would never have imagined they were both Silver-ranked. They glared silently at each other.

Recognizing how thoroughly unproductive the moment was, Female Knight finally came up and jabbed Heavy Warrior in the back of the head. "This is your fault, blast it."

"How is this my fault?"

"You're the one who tried to get a hand on that girl's older sister and her princess."

"I didn't try to *get a hand* on anything!" Heavy Warrior groaned. "Not on anyone's older sister and not on any princess."

Female Knight glared as if to say, *Excuse me?* Heavy Warrior could only sigh for the umpteenth time.

Bloodshed at a tavern was hardly unusual, but nobody wanted things to get out of hand. He'd given the tavern keeper a few coins for the trouble, left the centaur waitress to talk down her little sister, and made his retreat. He'd figured everyone would have cooled off by the next morning. And yet, now here he was.

He'd found Female Knight charging into his room in the morning, grabbing him by the nape of his neck, and dragging him to the Guild…

"And how exactly am I supposed to find this princess?" Heavy Warrior asked.

This one scruffy warrior was the only person he could turn to—what was he supposed to do? The high elf girl was watching the scene with undisguised amusement, while Dwarf Shaman seemed to be treating it as a show to accompany his meal. Heavy Warrior's accountant and the kids had promptly looked at him like a pariah and beaten feet.

Maybe if Spearman had been here…

Naw. He'd have laughed himself sick about this.

But Spearman wasn't an option, because he wasn't there. He and his partner were off on an adventure at the moment. Thank the gods.

"She's looking for a princess?" Goblin Slayer asked.

"That's what she says," Heavy Warrior replied.

"Hmm."

"I was just having a drink! I only said I was finally done sharpening my sword, and I could go on an adventure tomorrow."

"I see."

Heavy Warrior nodded at Goblin Slayer, who mumbled his various responses, and repeated: "I'm really not much for urban adventuring…"

"I see." The helmet shook again, and then the two men lapsed into silence. If left to their own devices, they seemed likely to go on like this forever, until the end of time.

Female Knight, however, had finally had enough. "Argh! We're not getting anywhere!"

Maybe it was her wish for an explanation that prompted Centaur Waitress to seize the moment. She clopped up to the group, holding her little sister by the hand—well, more like her sister refused to let go. "Uh, I'm sorry about her. Really."

"Sister! You don't have to apologize!" the younger centaur girl shouted, looking as if she might draw her sword at any moment. She was obviously not in the mood for discussion. "This man is at fault, and he alone!"

"See, this *is* all your fault," Female Knight said with a glare at Heavy Warrior, who stared helplessly up at the ceiling. He had never wished so desperately that the Supreme God would come and pass judgment himself. But the knight's deity had entrusted righteousness and justice and whatever else to humans. Maybe this was just another divine trial.

"Um…"

The Supreme God refused to intervene, but the Earth Mother stuck up for him.

"Maybe we could start by going over exactly what's happening. Slowly. From the beginning." Priestess was speaking to the centaur girl, nervously but not haltingly at all. Her collection of adventures and experiences had progressively shaped her into a real adventurer in her own right. "Fighting here is just going to cause trouble for everyone…"

Okay, so her motive wasn't deep compassion for Heavy Warrior—she cast a quick glance at the Guild reception desk. Guild Girl was standing there with a key in her hand and the kind of smile Heavy Warrior had never seen her make.

"She's quite right," said Guild Girl. "Perhaps you'd come talk over here?" Her language was so polite, yet it likewise brooked no argument.

Female Knight was on the move before Heavy Warrior could even try to stop her. "Yes, thanks, that sounds like a great idea."

"Not at all. Please let me know if I can be of help in any way." The key to the meeting room was reverently passed from Guild Girl's hand to Female Knight's.

"Okay, upstairs. You bunch of scoundrels..." Female Knight looked triumphant, grabbing Heavy Warrior's arm with a grip every bit as irrefutable as Guild Girl's pleasantries. That the Supreme God didn't see fit to punish her implied this was according to his will...

Looks like it's me against the world right now, Heavy Warrior thought. He nodded at Female Knight, looking like a prisoner about to be led to his execution.

§

"Okay, what's going on here?"

"Yes, do tell."

"Hey, don't ask me!" Heavy Warrior sank onto the bench, defeated, as High Elf Archer and Female Knight interrogated him, the elf's eyes shining and the knight's sharp as steel.

The meeting room on the second floor of the Adventurers Guild was by no means a small space—but with two centaurs and a lizardman crammed into it, it did start to feel a little claustrophobic. The room had been designed by humans, and although people of every kind came through the Guild, the builders probably hadn't designed the place with centaurs in mind. And if they had, then humans would probably have found the results pretty uncomfortable.

"Uh... Ha-ha... I'm sorry, y'know? Really," said Centaur Waitress, whose legs were bent uncomfortably in order to fit in her seat.

Lizard Priest, ever the gentleman, responded with a friendly nod.

"Goodness, fear not. You were simply dragged into this, it seems." But even the lizardman's decency couldn't spare him a glare from Centaur Waitress's younger sister, who still hadn't left her side.

Heavy Warrior had hoped the young woman might have come to her senses after spending the last night with her older sister, but she'd done nothing of the sort. In fact, she looked ready to draw her blade at any moment, as if she was poised to face down an army. In her mind, this was enemy territory, and she was right in the middle of it.

"Ever since last night, she hasn't stopped talking about how the princess is missing and she's come to find her," Centaur Waitress said, sounding downright hopeless.

"Hmm." Dwarf Shaman, who had been listening throughout the course of the conversation, grabbed a tipple and then asked, "This princess—she belongs to your people?"

"Yes, that's right. It's like…" Centaur Waitress made a gesture at the hair by her forehead, then traced it along her nose. "She had this one lock of white hair in her bangs. It looked like a silver star. Beautiful and awe-inspiring."

"And now she's gone?"

"She always was a bit of a tomboy—not that I'm one to talk! Ha-ha-ha!" Centaur Waitress laughed loudly, but even her attempt at cheerfulness couldn't take the edge off the atmosphere in the room.

"All right, out with it," Female Knight said, closing in on Heavy Warrior—even though this seemed less and less likely to have anything to do with him. At least, that's what the other adventurers thought (except maybe Goblin Slayer; it was hard to tell with him). They nodded at one another.

Only one person in the room knew what was really going on.

High Elf Archer turned her eyes with their starlike sparkle on the younger centaur. "Guess there's nothing for it but to…"

"…!"

"…ask you…" High Elf Archer trailed off, smiling ruefully at the brutal glare she received in return. She waved her hand dismissively, as if to say there was no hope here. If the centaur was willing to take that attitude even with a high elf, it at least proved that she didn't want for courage.

However, this was no way to have a conversation. And if they couldn't talk, then nothing was going to be solved. Just as they were trying to think of what to do:

"Um..."

There was a rustle of cloth, and as naturally as anything, Priestess was kneeling in front of the younger centaur. The centaur, who had knelt down on the carpet, yelped an "urk" and looked startled to find someone at eye level.

"I'm sure you're worried about your princess. But you can't figure out what to do on your own, can you?" Priestess asked.

"..."

The centaur didn't respond, but Priestess, taking this as confirmation, said, "I thought so." She nodded briefly and smiled. If the girl hadn't needed help, why would she have come all the way to an unfamiliar human settlement to seek out her older sister?

Priestess didn't say anything like, *It's okay* or *It'll be all right.* Instead, she whispered, "Come," and placed her palm atop the centaur girl's clenched fist. "Do you think you could tell us what's going on? Maybe we'll be able to help you somehow."

"......"

The girl remained silent for a long moment, meeting Priestess's blue eyes with a close-range glare, but finally she asked hesitantly, "How do you think you can do that, exactly?"

"Well, let's see...," Priestess said, putting a slim finger to her lips and looking theatrically thoughtful. "At the very least, if you'll share your story with us, we can all think about what to do together."

"......"

Once again, the centaur was silent. She looked at Priestess, who was waiting anxiously for her response, then at her older sister, standing to one side. Centaur Waitress brushed the girl's cheek, then let her hand run along her neck, as if to say, *Talk to them.* The girl's ears, flicking restlessly on top of her head, finally lay flat. "Fine," she said. "I'll talk."

Was that resignation in her voice or resolve? She clenched her fists, and her lips formed a single straight line. She thought silently for several moments, then began with no preamble: "......The princess set off from our *ulus*, our tribe, saying she was going to be an adventurer, and now we don't know where she is."

"Hmph. Hardly an uncommon story."

The sniff came from Female Knight, who still had Heavy Warrior cornered. For that matter, she still had him lifted up by the collar, and there was a striking quality of emotion in her voice. Only Priestess seemed to understand why, but she just smiled.

"Perhaps for you, but it's quite rare for us," the centaur girl said with a firm shake of her head that made her long ears and braided mane quiver and the sword and bow across her back tremble audibly. "What's more, the princess wasn't alone. She was tempted away by an adventurer."

"*This* adventurer?" Female Knight asked, lifting Heavy Warrior up even farther and eliciting a sound like a squished frog from him.

The girl studied him closely, then announced with absolute conviction: "The adventurer *was* carrying a greatsword."

"Well, there it is!" Female Knight said.

"There *what* is?" Heavy Warrior snapped. Then he added, "Let me go already!" He took her arm and twisted gently, and simple principles of body weight caused her grip to come open.

"Hrm," she growled, but Heavy Warrior was busy rubbing his neck.

"There must be a zillion adventurers who dress like me," he said, puffing out his cheeks at the idea that he might be the victim of a false accusation. "Lots of people carry broadswords—even if most of them are just hunks of metal."

"They're only imitating the saga—that black-clad swordsman's been a legend for a long time," Dwarf Shaman said easily, chuckling at the unusual sight of the despondent Silver.

Admittedly, the "black-clad swordsman" who had been so popular was supposed to have been an attractive man who wielded *two* blades, but times change. Nonetheless, it was still true that Heavy Warrior was among those who had attempted to follow in the swordsman's footsteps. How many adventurers, inspired by the way the legend made their pulses pound, had tried to trace its path, discover how it might end?

Now no one could know. Heavy Warrior had to realize that he would never reach that place, yet he still kept facing silently forward. He was an adventurer, and no matter how pathetic he might seem, how inexperienced, that was the only thing he could do.

"You just need to wear a helmet, like Orcbolg," High Elf Archer said, breaking the tension (purposely or not).

The centaur girl's palpable grief weighed on the room, and the elf's irrepressible cheerfulness was like a refreshing breeze blowing through. Hard to tell if she was acting on her comportment as a noble or whether it was something instinctive to high elves, but whatever the case, she drew a circle in the air with her pointer finger, the gesture immensely refined. "Then people wouldn't mistake you for anyone else."

"I was also told to always remember my helmet," Goblin Slayer muttered (a very earnest remark).

"Yeah?" Heavy Warrior replied.

There was wisdom, sometimes, in what the man in the grimy armor said, but at the moment, he didn't seem likely to be very helpful. In fact, Heavy Warrior suspected the rather troubled-looking cleric girl was his best bet. A couple or three years ago, she would probably have been standing there in a panic, but now she looked downright capable.

I guess the person herself is always the last to realize, Heavy Warrior reflected.

He thought of the kids in his own party and wondered if maybe he could stand to be a little tougher on them.

In any case, he shot Priestess a pointed look to keep things moving.

"Right," she said and nodded. "If that's all, then I'm not sure there's…anything we can do."

If the centaur girl wanted them to bring the princess back, that might be one thing. But if Priestess had been in a position to put people to work, she wouldn't have left things to this girl alone.

"Are you going to hire adventurers?"

When she remembered the hubbub surrounding the king's younger sister, Priestess quailed at the thought of having everything entrusted to her. She was not so simplistic, however, as to let those feelings show here and now. Instead, she maintained a serious demeanor and, in an attempt to get the centaur girl to keep talking, had spoken gravely to her.

"We haven't heard anything from her since then," the centaur girl said.

"It's possible..." *Possible she failed.* Not that Priestess would dare to say it aloud.

Adventurers took on dangerous quests—that was what made them adventurers. There was no quest that carried no danger of death. If you could just make money in complete safety doing this work, then who would hire adventurers for anything? No, be it slaying a dragon, mucking out the sewers, or hunting down goblins, danger was always at hand. It was sometimes greater and sometimes less—but even goblins, which were supposed to be the least threatening creatures in the world...

"Our princess was an accomplished fighter in her own right. Do you dare suggest that she would let herself be overcome like that?!" the centaur yelled reflexively, seeming to intuit what Priestess was thinking. "She never reached the point of going on an adventure! She was supposed to send word when she got to town, and she didn't even do that!"

"...I admit, that is a little strange," Priestess said.

The Four-Cornered World was full of adventure and danger, Fate and Chance—in the open field as much as anywhere. Okay, so maybe not everyone was going to bump into a dragon right on the road, but you could certainly have an unlucky encounter with a monster.

Still, this was a young woman who had gone to town in the company of a real adventurer, with hopes of becoming an adventurer herself. Would someone like that disappear without a trace, without asking anyone anywhere for help?

I think this could turn out to be quite the adventure, Priestess thought. Something far beyond a goblin hunt, whether it was the doing of monsters or people. She couldn't help hoping, though, that it might turn out to be nothing more than a simple case of a young woman running away from home. And that led to the hope that if that were so, the young woman might be reconciled to her family. Families weren't always lucky enough to get along well all the time, but there were better ways to take one's leave.

"Don't centaurs worry when the eldest daughter leaves the household?" Dwarf Shaman piped up, more or less ignoring Heavy Warrior, who was still being cornered by Female Knight, who was still convinced that he had somehow lured the girl into it. "I mean you and your princess both."

"Why should we worry? It's the youngest who inherits," Centaur Waitress said, as if it should have been obvious.

"A younger sister was born to the princess, so she was able to leave with no concern and no regrets," the waitress's sister added, equally blunt.

"Hoh," intoned Dwarf Shaman, impressed.

"Children are born stronger after bloodlines have already been joined," Centaur Waitress went on. "It doesn't settle everything, but that's how our *urus* thinks, at least."

"There are indeed many and varied customs," Lizard Priest said jovially.

"You're one to talk," High Elf Archer said with a bit of a smile. "Don't you kidnap your brides or something? I've got questions."

"What a thing to say." Lizard Priest's eyes rolled merrily in his head. He bared his fangs. "I have heard centaurs are the same way."

"Really?"

"Mm!" the centaur girl said with confidence, puffing out her toned chest proudly. "Obtaining an excellent spouse and making the bloodline ever stronger helps the tribe to glory and victory."

"The point is, this girl's the youngest, so she'll inherit our household," Centaur Waitress said. She poked her little sister in the forehead and teased, "What are you doing, dummy?"

"But, my honored sister!" the girl exclaimed, holding a hand to her brow. "I'm already an accomplished *baturu*! A warrior!"

She could protest that she was a centaur warrior-noble all she wanted, but it didn't change the fact that she was the youngest child.

"Dummy," her sister repeated and poked her again, this time eliciting an "ow!" from the accomplished warrior.

Female Knight and Heavy Warrior were jabbering away, as were Lizard Priest and High Elf Archer—and Dwarf Shaman, naturally, wasn't about to stop them. The somber atmosphere of moments ago was swept away, replaced by lively chatter and noise.

Goblin Slayer, who had been silent until then, watched the room for a moment and then said, "This is most familiar."

"Yep," said Priestess, who was watching everyone with something like pride. "All these youngsters who end up with us are like that—just nervous. Besides...," she added, "she's no scarier than a Viking." Priestess was making a joke, sort of—it was the truth, but not all of it.

Probably.

The centaur princess had gone missing, and this girl had come after her but had no one to turn to. Those were feelings Priestess could sympathize with. It was like being in a temple where you didn't know anyone, where you were forced to confront the fact that you were all alone in the Four-Cornered World. It was like supporting a wounded companion, leaving another of your friends screaming behind you as you crawled away through a dark cave.

Priestess knew in her skin the anxiety of such moments, the creeping terror.

"I see" was all Goblin Slayer said. He was silent for another moment, watching his friends and colleagues chatter boisterously. Priestess, sitting beside him, knew what he was thinking at such moments. Even if she couldn't see what was behind the visor of that grimy metal helmet. After a beat, he raised his head and said gravely, "...Do you think goblins are involved?"

Every gaze in the room shifted to him.

Goblin Slayer's helmet turned to take in Heavy Warrior, whom Female Knight had once again in her grasp. "I owe you a favor."

"I'm gonna owe *you* a favor by the time this is over." Heavy Warrior forced Female Knight's arms away again and resumed rubbing his neck, his lips turning up in a smile. "I'll pay you back sometime."

"Very well." Goblin Slayer nodded. "You'll have to treat me to a drink or the like. I believe that's the going rate." He thought for a moment; then his helmet tilted in curiosity. "But why me?"

"No other good scouts around."

"..." Goblin Slayer was silent for a moment, then said, "...I think of myself as a warrior."

High Elf Archer let out the sigh she'd been holding in, attracting a blank look from Baturu.

§

"My goodness, that sounds terrible!" Guild Girl exclaimed, and she wasn't being fatuous—this really was a serious matter.

An adventurer committing a kidnapping?

That was a problem. A big problem. A problem of blame. Who knew how far the ripples might reach?

The whole purpose of the Adventurers Guild was to certify that adventurers, so often regarded as riffraff and scoundrels, were nothing of the sort. That was the reason the country had gone out of its way to establish the Guild system. If people found out that the Guild had given its approval to someone who turned out to be a kidnapper, that would be a major issue. If it turned out to be someone from far away, who didn't know how things were done around here, they might be able to smooth things over, at least…

No, no!

Someone really was missing, so the very best they could hope for was that she would return unharmed.

"Anyway, all I can tell you is that there haven't been any centaurs who have registered as new adventurers recently." Guild Girl flipped through some records as she spoke.

"I see."

Centaurs stood out in a crowd. If one had been at the Guild, that alone would have been enough to get people talking.

Goblin Slayer nodded. "I should take that to mean that she isn't around here, then?"

"She didn't register as an adventurer here, at least."

But then, this town wasn't that big. If a centaur princess with a distinctive lock of silver hair on her forehead (so the centaur girl described her) was to show up here, somebody would have noticed. Which implied…

"I can't imagine she made it all the way to the capital," Guild Girl said. "But that still leaves—"

"The water town."

"Yes, exactly." Guild Girl nodded.

There were, of course, plenty of small villages and pioneer

settlements dotting the frontier where adventurers would be needed. But if a young centaur woman, taken with the idea of becoming an adventurer, had come here, there were likely only so many places she might have gone.

Maybe I'm stereotyping, but..., Guild Girl thought. It seemed to her that a centaur, whose people lived on the open plain, wouldn't be particularly impressed by life among frontier pioneers.

"I'd have to double-check to be completely certain, though. Let me have another look at the Adventurer Sheets," she said. She stood up and, after a moment's thought, added, "I'll also check for this adventurer who was supposedly wielding a broadsword."

"Yes, please," Goblin Slayer said.

"Of course." She smiled at him and then jogged back behind the curtain without ever looking anything less than refined and elegant.

Her colleague glanced up. Her face was stuffed full of sweets; whether she was on break or if this was a bit of slacking off was hard to tell. "What's up? Trouble?" she asked.

"They say an adventurer has vanished along with the person who came to town with him," Guild Girl replied.

"Blargh!" her colleague exclaimed, a sound not very fitting for either a disciple of the Supreme God or an employee of the Adventurers Guild. Admittedly, Guild Girl would have made the same sound if her position had permitted it. But it didn't.

Inspector stuffed the last of the treats in her mouth and washed them down with some dark tea, then said, "If our *more experienced* colleague found out about this, there'd be hell to pay." She didn't even try to hide her annoyance.

"She doesn't have to know."

"You've got that right." Naïveté.

Sometimes joking was the only way to cope.

In any case, Guild Girl was grateful to her friend, who immediately swept away the detritus of her snack and stood up. She pulled out the Adventurer Sheets of adventurers who had been active recently, and the two of them started flipping through the pages. A centaur adventurer and someone carrying a huge sword would both have stood out.

Goodness...

She discovered there was no shortage of adventurers who wanted to swing around a broadsword. Reasons varied: It was cool, or glorious, or it made them look strong, and so on. The fact that it wasn't just men but some women, too, maybe went to show the great glory of the Supreme God. Maybe.

Guild Girl thought she recalled songs about one of the six members of the All Stars being a warrior, a red-haired foreign mercenary who carried a massive blade.

I'm pretty sure she was a black-haired woman, wasn't she?

As Guild Girl scanned the pages, her eyes and hand and brain working, her mind cast away all extraneous thought.

"Mm, nothing here," Inspector said.

Guild Girl looked up when her colleague spoke, then added, "Looks like it." She nodded, closing a notebook. "Maybe she really did go to some other town."

"Yeah, probably." Inspector nodded as well, then stretched and put the papers back on the shelf. "I guess this is one of those things we'd better report to the Guild President, huh?"

"Could you handle that for me?" Guild Girl asked. A cleric of the Supreme God would be in a better position in a discussion like that.

"I don't mind—but I'd sure like to try using Sense Lie on this centaur girl." Inspector wiped some sweat from her brow as she finally finished reshelving all the papers. She looked very serious. "It's not that I think she's lying necessarily, but I need to be able to say I made sure."

"I understand that." Guild Girl smiled and giggled, brushing aside her braid, which had settled on her shoulder. She knew very well that her colleague wasn't drunk on power, wielding her authority in suspicion of everyone and everything. If she was that sort of person, Guild Girl doubted she would ever have received a miracle from the Supreme God. "I'll check with Goblin Slayer, but I think that should be all right."

Guild Girl reemerged at a quick jog, looking as energetic as a puppy; when she had explained the request to Goblin Slayer, he said, "I see," and nodded. "I don't believe she would listen if I asked her, but if the request came from our cleric, I doubt there would be a problem."

"Thank you so much. Given what's going on, I'll set things up so that this is a proper quest from the Guild." Part of it was that even Silver-ranked adventurers didn't work for free—but above all, it was because this incident affected the Guild's credibility. They would at least have to issue a survey quest. "I'll prepare a letter of introduction to the water town for you; you can show it to them when you arrive."

"Yes, please," Goblin Slayer replied.

Still...

Even as she industriously filled out paperwork and chatted with Goblin Slayer, Guild Girl couldn't suppress a smile. She knew it must seem out of place. She absolutely knew that this wasn't the time. Still. Yes, even so, and yet, it made her so happy.

"I think you've changed, Goblin Slayer," she said.

"How is that?" he asked.

"I mean..." Guild Girl held some paperwork in front of her to hide her smile; she looked as pleased as if she was speaking of herself. "You sound interested in an adventure involving something other than goblins."

"..."

You've become an outstanding adventurer. That was essentially what she'd said to him, but he only sank into a brief, almost sullen silence. Finally, he grunted and said, "...I don't see it."

§

"There's no need—*I* don't have to engage in such antics to know what I'm saying is the truth. If I know, that's enough."

"But don't you think if lots of people knew you were telling the truth, it would help you find your princess?"

"Hrm..."

"I know you can do it on your own—so just think of how much faster it'll go if everyone helps out!"

"Hrrrm..." Baturu's ears lay back on her head, and she nodded sweetly. If Priestess said so, then all right. Evidently the cleric had indeed been able to talk her around.

Such was the scene Goblin Slayer found upon returning to the

©Noboru Kanna

waiting area. He was sincerely pleased to find it had been the right choice to let Priestess handle the young woman.

"Even dwarves and lizardmen usually freak out when they see something they think is a Living Armor," High Elf Archer said, kicking her legs in amusement and squinting like a cat. "But you can even stare down a high elf. Truly, a fearless centaur warrior."

"Hrmph," grunted Baturu, sticking out her lip at the elf's gentle teasing. She glared at the adventurer. "I'm told that your kind trick people into getting lost in the forest, then ambush them with a hail of stones from the treetops. They say you can't be too careful around elves."

"Sure they weren't talking about some other sort of faerie?" High Elf Archer guffawed and waved the story away, despite the exasperated look on her face. "Anyway, it doesn't matter. There's going to be a formal quest, and we've accepted it. Now you can just leave it to the adventurers!"

"I'm not saying I trust you," the centaur said with a pout. "I'm going, too."

"That is *not* a demand the inheritor of our family's estate gets to make," Centaur Waitress said. There was a *gong!* as she smacked Baturu on the head; Baturu clutched her brow and exclaimed, "Ow!" Centaur Waitress snorted and glared at her, but her expression quickly softened. Her personality, along with her experience, must have been what enabled her to switch between domestic scolding and external politeness so quickly. "Unfortunately, I know that once this girl says she's going to do something, she won't listen to reason, so if you don't mind..." She bowed her head respectfully.

"Mm, mm," Lizard Priest said with a broad wave—a sign of acceptance. Sometimes such a deferential attitude was part of responding appropriately to another person's feelings. Centaur Waitress would have only grown more anxious if the adventurers about to take her little sister away had acted too humble or lacking in confidence. "We shall do whatsoever is within our power. You may set your mind at ease."

"Thank you. I'm worried about the princess, too. I hope you all can find out what's going on," Centaur Waitress said. "C'mon, you too," she added in the direction of Baturu, who dipped her head reluctantly.

"Thank you for your help," she said, failing to successfully hide the displeasure in her voice. An argument broke out between the sisters: the elder exclaiming, "Be nice!" and the younger retorting, "I said it, didn't I?!" Their disagreement was noisy, but Goblin Slayer was silent as he watched the sisters jabber at each other. He said nothing, nor even began to say anything. He didn't even grunt softly, as he usually did. No one in the party could guess what expression he was making under that metal helmet.

"How about it, Beard-cutter? What d'you plan to do?" Dwarf Shaman asked, judging the most natural timing.

"Hrm...," Goblin Slayer muttered, as if only now registering the presence of others. His helmet moved. "What do I plan to do about what?"

"I mean, what're you going to do next?"

"Ah..."

Surely he'd at least been considering it, but Goblin Slayer crossed his arms as if in thought.

A missing princess. An adventurer who might have kidnapped her. Located in the water town.

No communication since the princess's disappearance—it would have taken a few days before this centaur girl decided to act. Long enough that if the princess was in mortal danger, they should assume it was now too late.

But what if it wasn't?

"We need to hurry, but it'll be quicker to catch tomorrow's first carriage than to walk," he said.

"Good point. We won't be needin' provisions, but have you got that letter of introduction to the water town office?" Dwarf Shaman asked.

"Mm." Goblin Slayer nodded. "And I have acquaintances in that city. We'll manage."

"You mean Lady Archbishop," Dwarf Shaman said. "And that young woman. I hear she's doing quite well for herself in the world of commerce."

Priestess picked up the thread: "She's been at the king's palace pretty much all the time lately!" She sounded as pleased as if she was talking about herself.

"Sounds like she's keeping busy," High Elf Archer said with a twitch of her ears. "Why do you humans like to collect money so much? It's just round pieces of metal."

"It lets you have good wine and good food, even if you can't make 'em yourself. That's the power of cash." Dwarf Shaman nodded knowingly and took a swig of fire wine from the gourd flask at his hip. "Money helps you manage what you can't do on your own. It's pretty convenient once you grasp the principle."

"Huh. Is that how it works?"

"*You've* got money," Dwarf Shaman said, scowling at the elf. "That's why you can blow it playing around!"

"Sure, sure… Wait, I'm not blowing it!" The elf tried waving away the hurtful words with an indeterminate gesture; the remark seemed to hurt even her long ears.

"…You speak of *jiaochao*, yes?" Baturu said with a serious expression, her hooves clapping on the floor. She seemed to feel this was the perfect excuse to escape her sister's lecture. "It appears you are going to help us, much as I might wish it were not so. I am more than willing to compensate you." (Then again, perhaps it was her older sister's presence that made her try to act as mature as possible.) Ignoring Centaur Waitress's slight smile, Baturu reached into her baggage and pulled out a pouch. "How much will it be? Will this be enough?"

She held it up proudly. Dwarf Shaman took it in his fingers, his eyes going wide. "I can't believe this…"

It was a bill. A paper bill, made from some sort of grass ("Mulberry skins," High Elf Archer commented). It was a sight to behold, covered in letters and elaborate patterns in ink.

But that was all it was. High Elf Archer might not have realized it, but Priestess did; she said, "Er, *ahem*," and looked uncomfortable.

Baturu flicked her tail in annoyance at the uneasy looks from all and sundry. "What, you need more?"

"We need currency we can use!" Dwarf Shaman said. "I mean, sure, good paper has its value—but paper's not gold or silver." He held the bill near a lantern so the light shone through it, and he shook his head.

"…You barbarians," Baturu spat and snatched the bill back.

Centaur Waitress—who had certainly seen this coming—was about to offer a sisterly word of exasperation, but then Goblin Slayer said, "It makes no difference to me. A reward has already been promised, and I don't seek more than that."

"...Are you sure, sir?" Centaur Waitress asked.

"I meant what I said," Goblin Slayer replied. Before Centaur Waitress or Baturu could speak up again, he cast a look around at everyone in the room and said, "Come what may, we leave tomorrow. You should all go get ready."

§

Who talks like that? It was almost as if I was...their leader, Goblin Slayer mused, chastising himself. He was on the way home, and the gore-red light of the setting sun turned the town orange and shimmered over the path to the farm. He walked nonchalantly, weaving among the people around him, making his way through a scene he'd experienced many times before.

Knowing there was some part of him that was pleased was deeply discomforting.

An adventurer... Didn't it make him nervous to be seen as one?

I fear I'll cease to pay attention to where I'm going.

He must never begin thinking that he was somehow special. He must simply remember that he had done all he could do and that this was where it had led him. That was the simple fact; he was neither contemptuous nor envious of anyone else.

And yet, it bothered him that no one had pushed back against the words he had spoken earlier.

Were their perceptions changing with time, leaving him behind? Was what they were seeing really *him*? Could it be that after years of pulling the wool over their eyes, he was going to be seen through at a stroke? Realize that he had his hands full simply handling whatever was in front of him—that that was the most he could manage?

Hmm.

Did that mean he wished to be thought of as someone important? Someone special?

What a ridiculous idea. Truly and profoundly stupid.

The very fact that he was even expending any energy thinking about this was the height of foolishness.

"...It's very difficult," he said slowly. A quest searching for a centaur princess was the last thing he was suited for. And when he thought about it, he realized:

Quests like that seem to have become my bread and butter lately. From running the dungeon exploration contest to surveying the northern reaches—even, going back a bit, the exploration of the underground city. *When this is over,* he thought, *I'll focus on goblin hunting for a while.*

Goblin hunting was certainly no picnic (nor was any adventure). But everyone had specific strengths and weaknesses, just like how Heavy Warrior said he wasn't suited to urban adventuring. From that perspective, goblin hunting was good. There were fewer things you didn't know, fewer things to worry about—like what was where or what would happen in the next instant. Goblin nests were familiar places to Goblin Slayer. They almost felt like home.

Now that I think about it...

It occurred to him that he had now spent longer in goblin nests than he had in his own village. At the realization, he felt his lips tighten, tensing into a warped smile beneath his helmet.

That was living; that was all it was. It didn't always go the way you wanted.

"...You're back?"

He halted, surprised by the voice that came at him from the dusk. A figure stood outlined by the brackish sunlight—the owner of the farm.

"Yes," he answered after a moment's thought. Then he added in a respectful tone, "I was thinking about what I would do on my next adventure." It sounded like an excuse. The owner hadn't asked him about that.

The man was swinging a farm implement listlessly through some hay. In the middle of fieldwork, perhaps. He sighed and hefted his pitchfork onto his shoulder with a motion that suggested it was a great effort. "Another goblin hunt?" he asked.

"No, sir," Goblin Slayer replied. After a moment of thought, he shook his head. "It doesn't seem to be." Then he even added that he had been asked to find someone.

He said nothing further—he couldn't. He didn't know how to explain it. How to tell the other man that he had been asked to find a centaur princess, just as if he was a halfway decent adventurer. He accepted that some people might laugh in his face if they heard it, not that he thought this man to whom he owed so much would necessarily do so.

"That right...?" The owner almost looked relieved. Although Goblin Slayer didn't understand why he would feel that way. "Tough job?"

"I'm afraid I don't know yet."

He refrained from mentioning that it would depend on the circumstances. That the most optimistic scenario was that the centaur princess had simply forgotten to send her letter after she left home and was now an adventurer in the water town. That was still not outside the realm of possibility, so he would have to investigate before he could say anything for sure.

Baturu was adamant that the princess wouldn't have been so neglectful of her commitments, but...

I'm not so sure.

They would get nowhere except by testing each possibility, one thing at a time.

"She doesn't appear to be in this area, however," Goblin Slayer continued. "I think I'll end up going to the water town."

"I see..."

The owner and Goblin Slayer started walking side by side. It wasn't far to the main house. The owner was probably on his way to put his tools in the shed (not the one Goblin Slayer was using). Goblin Slayer didn't expect the conversation to last terribly long.

"Things'll get busier by the end of summer," the owner said. "If you were back by then, it'd be a help."

"Yes, sir."

He shuffled along beside the man, feeling like a child whose parents were asking him to help out. He found it hard to claim that he was particularly good at farmwork, especially with this seasoned professional right next to him, but he'd picked up the basics.

Moving his body without having to think was relaxing for him. He would never keep up with people if he constantly had to be using his wits. He was convinced he was more suited for work that didn't require such mental exertion.

"I'll do what I can," he said.

He wasn't sure what the old farmer thought about that, but the man said, "Ah… I didn't mean it like that. I didn't mean you have to hurry your work…"

The door to the main house was before them, but Cow Girl, whose cooking was presumably the source of the smoke drifting from the chimney, wouldn't be able to hear them from here. The farm owner stopped and looked at Goblin Slayer's metal helmet. Finally, he said slowly, "Work is work. Someone asked you to do it, and you accepted, yes?"

"Yes, sir."

"Then make sure you do it right."

From behind his visor, Goblin Slayer looked at the farmer. The farmer gazed back, straight at him, as if his armor wasn't there.

"They'll know if you cut corners," the man said.

"…Yes, sir."

Thick hands covered in dirt and scratches gave Goblin Slayer's leather armor a gentle pat. Goblin Slayer watched the old man as he walked away toward the storehouse. He let his own fingers brush the dust where the farmer's hand had touched his shoulder.

He was convinced his own hands would never be like that.

§

"So you're leaving again?"

"Seems like it."

She knew he must be nodding his helmeted head from his place at the table behind her. Cow Girl always loved these quiet moments when the two of them were alone together as she got dinner ready.

I guess Uncle is nice enough to leave us alone…

The thought made her feel embarrassed, or maybe a little shy, so she determined not to think about it.

A pot of stew, rich with milk, was heating on the stove; she stirred it idly from time to time. The smoke from the stove and the steam from the pot combined to feel warm and friendly. The dishes and tableware had been polished with cleaning sand until they gleamed; it was as if they were eagerly waiting for their turn to serve.

She couldn't wait, either. This was one of the moments she loved most of all.

He liked stew very much—and she liked serving it to him. Besides, a farmer's dinner was supposed to be stew; it was practically a cliché. Only in the city did you get to have rich, elaborate fare for every meal. A city like…

"The water town, say?"

"Mm."

She'd almost been talking to herself, but he responded nonetheless.

Cow Girl smiled happily, just as glad that her back was to him.

"I don't know how long it will take, though."

"No?"

"I'll be looking for someone," he said. "It won't be over until I find them."

"Sounds tough…," she said, although she didn't have any idea how tough it might actually be. Once, she had visited an elf village (ah, that had been like a dream!). And not long before, she had been attacked by goblins in an abandoned village in winter (ah, that had been like a nightmare!). But this alone didn't give her any understanding of the difficulties of real adventure, let alone doing something someone had requested you to do. That, she knew only from what he'd told her.

"But I'd like to try to finish the quest and be back before the end of summer," he added.

"Sure." She nodded, giving the stew a stir. It wasn't that big a deal. She thought she understood, more or less, what he was trying to say. But rather than point it out, she often liked to wait silently. She kept one eye on him as she glanced at the meal or opened and closed the cupboard to no real purpose.

Still wearing his metal helmet as he always did, her childhood friend continued slowly. "So I'll be away again starting tomorrow."

He stopped there and fell into something of a sullen silence. It did not signal the end of the conversation—that much she had learned long ago. So she simply looked down into the pot, considering what she would say, how she would answer…

"I'll be back," he said finally.

"Have a good trip," she replied. She hoped her voice hadn't scratched as she spoke. She wasn't sure. His own voice had been tenser than usual; he seemed to speak all in a single rushing breath.

"…"

At last, Cow Girl couldn't stand just stealing sidelong glances and turned to face him. She rested on the edge of the stove, almost sitting on it (not very polite of her), and looked at him. He was sitting silently at the table, looking straight back at her.

She peered behind his visor. She knew the expression that must be on his face, as if she could see it with her own eyes.

The canary chirped faintly from a corner of the house.

Cow Girl was the first to speak at the sound, unable to hold it in any longer. "…I guess this isn't exactly the time for this conversation, huh?" she said, giggling.

"Mm," he replied and nodded very seriously. "Although I wasn't sure how else to say it."

"Me neither!" Now laughing out loud, she turned back toward the stew. Her uncle would be coming in for dinner soon. It would be the last time they ate together as a family for a while.

Maybe I should have made something fancier, she thought.

But he liked stew, and she liked to make it for him. It would be a while until she got to do that again, too—and the thought made her feel that "the usual" was best tonight.

A pleasant aroma wafted from the stew; it would taste wonderful and be hearty in their stomachs.

He'll have to go without this for a while…

That was part of what made adventuring so tough, she figured. That struck her as less than modest, and she started laughing again.

Would it have been too ordinary to tell him to be careful? *Do your best!* meanwhile, seemed somehow irresponsible. Wasn't he always doing the best he could?

Cow Girl let her imagination range as she spooned the stew into their bowls. She thought about how she would spend the time until he got back; she wondered whether her uncle already knew about this trip.

The water town: She'd been there once before. It was a big city. He had gone a number of times, by her recollection.

Oh yeah! Even as she chatted with him, Cow Girl's mind didn't stop working. There were things she had to do. Such as, say…

"You're welcome to bring me a souvenir—but no animals this time, okay?"

"…" He grunted softly, then tilted his head, perplexed. "I don't think I bring you animals that often."

Just doing what had to be done each day as she waited for him would be work enough.

§

"…I will *not* ride in any vehicle pulled by horses!"

Well, they probably should have seen that coming.

It was the next morning, and they were at the carriage station on the outskirts of the frontier town. Warm sunlight shone down on people heading east to the capital and those going even farther west, toward the pioneer settlements. Some of the travelers appeared to be farming families with their lives on their backs, while others were mountaineers carrying digging equipment.

Merchants with loads of cargo, preachers with holy books, and a circuit-rider woman were all there, too. As, of course, were the adventurers in their panoply of equipment who served as bodyguards to all these. Boots, hooves, and of course carriage wheels clattered over the flagstones. There was a lively burble of conversation.

The place was small for a station, but it was still the most crowded spot in town. And standing there, making an unwavering declaration about her willingness (or not) to ride in a wagon, was the young centaur woman Baturu. She stared with astonishment at the horses hitched to the wagon, who were taller than she was.

"T'ain't going to get there by walking," said Dwarf Shaman, who had worked his proverbial magic to arrange the ride. In fact, he cut quite a dashing figure sitting in the driver's seat, holding the reins.

"Wow, you rented this for us?" Priestess asked him.

"Figured it'd be a lot more convenient than sharing a ride."

To Priestess, the horse looked in excellent shape, its legs large and strong, its mane shiny, its eyes glittering. She patted its nose, and it gave her palm a friendly nuzzle. Priestess smiled at it.

"It looks very smart and very strong… It would probably be fit for riding," she said.

The wagon Dwarf Shaman had procured was just as magnificent, a large vehicle with a cover. It seemed like maybe it was intended to carry cargo rather than passengers—but the wheels looked a little elaborate for that…

"It's for transporting wine," Dwarf Shaman explained when he saw Priestess looking at the wheels. "And shaking is the enemy of good wine." He grinned mischievously. "After what happened with the early harvest and the sacred drink, I thought the wine merchant might be open to negotiating. Let's just say I borrowed this thing."

"Ahhh…"

Priestess was surprised to realize that she now looked back almost fondly on the events to which he was referring. The commotion surrounding the sacred wine—some things about it had been unpleasant, but as adventures went, everything had ended more or less happily. She remembered Sister Grape had been quite close with the young merchant.

I guess those are important connections, too. Who knew when they might come in handy on an adventure? She nodded to herself: She would have to remember that.

"I don't need this!" Baturu declared, otherwise ignoring the conversation between Dwarf Shaman and Priestess. She was scuffing the ground angrily, as if to communicate that she wanted to leave *right now.* The stone felt so different under her hooves than the grass of the field, and that only made her more upset. "I'm perfectly capable of walking the distance to the water town or wherever it is. Unlike you humans."

"Why make things harder when you can make them easier?" said High Elf Archer, peering out from under the wagon cover, into which she had slithered almost without their noticing. She'd already staked out her spot, tossing her baggage down and kicking back.

She must have caught some provocation from Dwarf Shaman on the driver's seat, because her ears went flat; she pulled her head back under the cover and shouted, "I can hear you, dwarf!" after which she reemerged. "That's one human philosophy I think we can learn from," she said before adding, "because humans are experts at being lazy!" Even the way she cackled sounded like a tinkling bell.

"I don't think it's laziness…," Priestess offered, but all she could do was smile.

She tried finding an angle where she could meet Baturu's eyes, just like she had the day before, but unlike when the other girl had been sitting down, she now had a head's height on Priestess. Stretch and stand on her tiptoes how she might, Priestess couldn't look Baturu in the eyes; she finally resorted to climbing on a wooden crate.

When Baturu saw that, her head drooped slightly, although Priestess didn't look much happier. "I suppose it's…not impossible. Horses are horses. They're not Pray-ers…"

It was much like how a human felt no particular discomfort watching a monkey being made to perform. (Although in fairness, the idea that humans and monkeys shared some kind of blood relationship was just one of those absurd things the lizardmen were given to saying…)

"However, is it not the height of folly to entrust oneself to another's back?" Baturu asked.

"There is indeed something compelling to that logic," Lizard Priest said, slithering down to look under the wagon. His trained warrior's eyes would not miss anything that had gone unprepared. He and Goblin Slayer appeared satisfied with their inspection of the vehicle. It wasn't that they didn't trust the wine merchant or, for that matter, Dwarf Shaman, but there was always the possibility of problems that no one had even thought of.

"For example, I was veritably freezing during our battle in the water," Lizard Priest went on. His blood, he informed them, had quite slowed down! He sounded like he was making some kind of joke, but lizardman humor could be hard to fathom. It must have been uncomfortable, though, knowing that his entire fate rested in the hands of others.

"All the more reason for me to walk…!" Baturu said.

"But it won't do you any good to waste your stamina," Goblin Slayer replied as he dusted off his gloves, evidently finding the state of the wagon acceptable. "A human can cover a hundred kilometers by walking two nights through, but we use horses."

"Hrm…" Baturu looked like she wanted to say something to that but couldn't think up a comeback; all she could do was grumble. Could centaurs not manage that speed, then? For that matter, could humans?

Priestess looked from Baturu to Goblin Slayer and back, then finally just asked the question: "…Is that true?"

"A human can match a horse for speed—at least over a long distance like that," Goblin Slayer answered.

In short sprints, a horse or a centaur could use their explosive power—literal horsepower—to be much faster than a human. Across long distances, meanwhile, a human could prevail using their most ordinary trait: almost inexhaustible stamina. In the Four-Cornered World, humans were, after all, recognized as the most tenacious people, those who were the worst at knowing when to give up.

"That, however, is assuming one kept nothing in reserve. If you want to be ready for a fight, then you must conserve what you're able," Goblin Slayer said.

Right.

Priestess gripped her sounding staff firmly with both hands and nodded. "If you can win by doing something reckless or outrageous, then it makes things easier… Like you always say!"

Goblin Slayer was silent. High Elf Archer was on the wagon's luggage rack, grinning like a cat. Baturu, unsure what that was supposed to mean, simply looked confused.

Goblin Slayer grunted quietly, and then before Priestess or anyone else could say anything, he continued in a quick, low tone. "…There is also the rain and the wind to consider. And neither you nor I wish to remove our armor, yes?"

Here, too, Baturu seemed to have no answer.

Priestess could only imagine a life of running free around grassy fields—but she was familiar with the elements, for she had encountered them many a time on her adventures. Not just wind and rain—she had found herself faced with snow and storms as well. Older and more experienced adventurers had warned her not to be cavalier about even a passing shower. Someone might say to themselves that it was only a little rain, and the next town was close, and they would just get wet as they walked there—only to collapse by the road and die. Yes, it could happen in the rain, not just in blizzards. One never knew what Fate and Chance held in store.

Baturu must have been well acquainted with the cruelties of nature.

"........Fine," she said at last. "Yes, I understand." She puffed out her cheeks like a young woman scolded by her parents or teacher. "I am not enough of a child to keep griping."

She trotted over to the wagon (*clop, clop*), where she reared up and put her front legs on the cart. High Elf Archer quickly reached out and took her hand to help her, but even for a high elf, a centaur was heavy. Priestess quickly moved to support Baturu's rear end—but then realized she wasn't sure how to help.

"Uh, m-may I touch you here...?" she asked.

"...Yes, that's fine."

So with some hesitation, Priestess pushed on Baturu's shapely buttocks. It wouldn't have bothered her to do this to a horse, but she was dealing with a centaur—with a toned young woman, at that. She looked at the ground to hide the flush in her cheeks; the velvety feeling under her hands gave her the sense that she was doing something wrong. She couldn't see Baturu's face, but maybe that was for the better.

"And...hup!" Baturu said.

The sight of a centaur clambering into a wagon must have been a strange one indeed, for many passersby at the station turned and gawked. A glare from Lizard Priest, however, persuaded them to go about their business.

Thankfully, Baturu was able to make her way onto the wagon readily enough, if not quite gracefully. However, even the relatively spacious vehicle felt a little cramped with a centaur the size of a young horse in it. It didn't help that, though she ducked to fit under the cover, she remained standing. High Elf Archer looked perplexed, but Lizard Priest stuck his head under the wagon cover and said, "I was unsure what the centaurs do in such situations, you see. Shall I bring straw for you?"

"...I'm not a horse," the young centaur lady replied brusquely, making no effort to hide the annoyance on her face. She nonetheless didn't completely abandon her civility, seeing as Lizard Priest did behave as if he was dealing with nobility. Humans had a tendency to view lizardmen and centaurs (to say nothing of frontierspeople) as simple barbarians, yet here they were.

"Forgetting your manners when the other person could kill you at any moment would be to take your life in your hands," Lizard Priest had said. And yet, Priestess sometimes found herself thinking that his lack of hesitation as he said this perhaps showed that he was the more civilized.

"We lay a *khivs* on the floor of our *ger* for rugs," Baturu said. "But... since there is no *khivs* here, straw will do."

"Splendid," Lizard Priest said.

"I'll go get some!" Priestess offered, and then she set off, pattering along like a small bird. There must have been some straw close by a station like this.

Goblin Slayer watched her go, full of vim and vigor and downright excitement at the idea of an adventure. Then he hefted the bag she'd left onto the luggage rack. He studied Baturu closely from behind his visor (she made a small "erk") and headed for the driver's bench. As the scout charged with keeping an eye out for enemies as they made their way across the open plain, it would be best for him to be somewhere with a wide, open field of view. It was always Goblin Slayer's role to switch off with High Elf Archer, each of them keeping their eyes peeled in turn.

Using the step, he swung himself up beside Dwarf Shaman, looking accustomed to the act if not quite graceful.

"Ho, Beard-cutter. This is shaping up to be quite an adventure."

"An adventure..."

"Sure! Finding a lost princess! Though I've got to say...you don't hear much about centaurs in the sagas." He grinned and offered a sip of fire wine to Goblin Slayer, who silently declined. "No?" Dwarf Shaman asked, but he accompanied it with a great guffaw, not upset in the least. He took a dramatic swig himself.

Finally, wiping the droplets off his beard with his sleeve and lighting up his red face with a smile, he said, "...Disappointed it's not goblins?"

"No," was all Goblin Slayer told him.

Goblin Slayer shook his head and looked around at the mass of people going by. They chatted amiably under the bright sunlight; boots smacked against flagstones, almost as if pushing their owners forward through town. Some of them were leaving the Adventurers Guild, checking their equipment, chatting with their party members, clad in every manner of gear as they headed out. They belonged to every race and age and job and gender, those who walked by, and not one of them doubted where their road was leading.

Not one of them went forward assuming they would fail on their next adventure.

If one wanted only to earn money to survive, one could just as easily be a farmer or, for that matter, a prostitute. There were plenty of options. If one wanted only to achieve victory and earn glory, one could be a knight, a mercenary, or a sword fighter.

There was something else. Something those vocations didn't have. That was what drove people to risk themselves on adventures. That was what made them adventurers. If they didn't seek that thing, they wouldn't be adventurers.

"..." The One Who Slays Goblins sighed. "I think...perhaps it might be good to try something else."

"Well, you *were* personally asked. Got every reason to hold your chest high and do it."

"That's easy enough to say."

Dwarf Shaman didn't reply but waited patiently for Goblin Slayer's next words. High Elf Archer, under the cover, could probably hear what they were saying, but she chose not to interject. What about Lizard Priest? One couldn't be sure, but in any case, he busied himself dealing with Baturu.

Goblin Slayer was painfully grateful for his party members' decorum.

He sighed. How, he wondered, could he repay them for that?

"…But it is difficult," he eventually said.

"Ah, there ain't an easy adventure around," Dwarf Shaman agreed. And he was right.

Priestess came jogging back with an armful of straw, her brow glistening with sweat. "Thanks for waiting!" she said.

Goblin Slayer nodded, contemplated what he ought to say, and then spoke it:

"Very well. Let's go."

CHAPTER 2

Stay Away From Goblins!

"What? You can keep those lumpy donkeys even on your grassy fields?" Priestess asked.

"...It's called a camel," Baturu said.

The girls' conversation was almost as noisy as the clacking of the wagon wheels.

It had started when— Well, what *had* started it? Priestess had talked to Baturu, had kept bringing the conversation back to her, while Baturu gave curt responses. This had gone easily enough as they left town and got out into the open field. It was too soon to say Baturu had opened up to Priestess, but already she was no longer driving her away.

Gradually, oh so gradually, approaching someone's heart—that was Priestess's way. Something she had learned from her training at the Temple of the Earth Mother.

Or maybe more accurately, it's just the way she is, High Elf Archer thought idly from her place beside Lizard Priest on the driver's bench.

Humans matured so quickly. You looked away for a second, and suddenly they had grown up. In High Elf Archer's eyes, at least, the little girl who used to cower before goblin hunts was gone. Whether or not she herself realized it, she had become a proper adventurer.

"...They provide hair and even milk. And they're essential for carrying things."

On top of Priestess's natural personability, there was the unmistakable fact that Baturu was looking for a way to feel a bit better. She was out in the field, under the open sky, yet she was trapped beneath a cover, squeezing down so she could fit. To be unable to feel the wind against her skin must have been intolerable for a centaur.

Above all, who wouldn't be happy to have someone inquire sweetly and innocently about their home? Spotting the opportunity and smoothly beginning a conversation—that was one of Priestess's strengths.

She probably just thinks she's "trying her best."

"Carrying things...?"

A sudden, startling whisper could be heard amid the rattling of the wagon. It came from Goblin Slayer, who was sitting on a corner of the luggage rack now that he had traded guard duty with High Elf Archer. It was hard to even tell if he was awake or asleep under that helmet.

Baturu had almost forgotten about the suit of armor; the way the voice emerged from it so abruptly sent a shiver through her ears and tail.

"That thing has humps. It can't be easy to pile items on it," Goblin Slayer said.

"I-it's not that hard..." Baturu couldn't hide the initial scratch in her voice despite the noise of the vehicle. "You simply wrap a *tereg*, a cotton cloth, between the humps and pass a *shata*, a structural frame, through it. It forms an excellent and stable place for goods."

"In between the humps?" Goblin Slayer grunted softly. "It only has one hump, does it not?"

"No, two," Baturu replied. "You're not making any sense."

"Hmm..." Goblin Slayer fell into silent thought for a moment, then said quickly, "How do you handle them?"

"We use a *morin khuur*. It has a calming effect on camels."

"*Morin khuur.*"

"It's a musical instrument. Exactly what kind..." Baturu moved her hands in the air, sketching out the shape of the instrument, but her ears sat back on her head. "...I can't quite describe."

"I see," Goblin Slayer said, and then he went quiet again. Baturu watched him suspiciously, unsure whether the conversation was over.

Ah, Priestess thought, a giggle escaping her. She could easily picture the camel they kept on the farm. If Dwarf Shaman was playing possum (did they even have possums in this part of the world?), he must have noticed it, too—and if that was why he was keeping quiet…

"And how do you use a camel's milk and hair?" Priestess, suspecting she was supposed to make the next move, asked Baturu.

"Well… When you think of camels, you think of *airag*."

"Um… Which means…?"

"It's an alcohol made from milk. But on its own, it's very sour, so we add sugar and distill it as well."

Priestess offered a genuinely impressed "ahhh." She wondered if Lizard Priest could hear them from the driver's seat. He would no doubt find the subject very interesting.

It wasn't clear what Baturu made of Priestess's reaction, but she chuckled. "So you know about distilling. I wasn't sure you had the technology here."

Yes, Priestess knew—although she didn't say so. She knew *about* it, but she didn't actually know how it was done. In her mind, it was akin to alchemy. She was sure a cleric of the God of Knowledge, or perhaps of Wine, would know all about it. Or maybe a follower of the sadistic god like the *húsfreya* up north… But they didn't have one of those around.

Anyway…

"It's really amazing that you're able to do that out on the plain," she said.

"Well, it does require some tools," Baturu replied.

Anyway, this wasn't the place for an intellectual pissing contest. And Priestess really was genuinely impressed.

"Then there's hair," Baturu said. She seemed to be in better spirits now, her cheeks flushing and the words coming more and more readily. "Camel hair. It's very good stuff, soft and thick. We make thread from it and use it for weaving."

"It sounds so different from sheep's wool," Priestess offered.

"It's completely different," Baturu said. She didn't seem to realize the expression that had been on her face until that moment, but she suddenly appeared to think she had talked too much. "Completely different," she repeated, looking away pointedly.

For crying out loud, High Elf Archer thought. She found the entire scene amusing, fun, and endlessly exciting. She grabbed a leaf that came fluttering by on the wind and put it to her lips, blowing through it to create a rich sound that carried up to the sky.

"You're quite good at that," Lizard Priest commented.

High Elf Archer opened her mouth just enough to say, "Eh, y'know," her long ears flicking, looking like leaves themselves.

She grinned like a cat at the way Lizard Priest rolled his eyes merrily beside her, then bit down on the leaf. Swinging her leg, which hung lazily from the driver's bench, there under the blue sky she played a melody that seemed beyond anything that should be able to come from a simple leaf. It grabbed the attention of everyone under the cover—Baturu and all the adventurers—as well as every living thing in the wide field outside. In the hands of a high elf, it seemed, even a grass flute could produce the music of heaven. It was calm, peaceful, and warm; all the Four-Cornered World seemed to bless her and her music then.

It was one of those rare moments, like floating on the surface of water, that seemed as if it would go on forever. Even elves, with their nigh-immortal life spans, did not meet many moments like this.

Time itself might be without end, but the time we can spend with those we love is limited. Thus, the only thing that could bring an end to this scene would be the arrival at their destination…

"Ohhh, for—!"

…or if something happened that she certainly did not wish.

Frowning mightily and releasing her leaf back to the wind, High Elf Archer stood up on the driver's bench. The first to react was Goblin Slayer, who had been sitting silently listening to her play. He clasped the sword at his hip, sat up, and asked sharply: "Goblins?"

"Sadly," High Elf Archer cried, casting aside any high elf–ish elegance, "you're right!"

§

"If we had to have a random encounter, I wish it could've been a dragon!" High Elf Archer exclaimed.

"Yes, it might indeed be quite interesting to be annihilated by one!" Lizard Priest said.

High Elf Archer managed to climb up on top of the wagon cover while she was complaining; Lizard Priest snapped the reins and laughed.

The wagon bounced down the road, going...well, not like the wind, exactly. And they could definitely see enemies around. They were only goblins, though, and couldn't possibly catch a wagon on foot.

"GROOORGB!!"

"GBOG! GRORGB!!"

"GRBBB!!"

If they'd stolen the secret of riding, however, that was different.

The goblins rode clinging to the backs of their wolves—really, wargs—slowly but surely closing the gap. Did they somehow communicate with the fell canines, or did they simply hold the reins and hope for the best? That might forever remain a mystery, but *goblins* was still a dangerous word nevertheless.

Dwarf Shaman glared back out from under the wagon cover, though the frown on his face didn't stop him from sipping his fire wine. "Maybe your whistling drew 'em here," he said.

"Yeah, sure. Or maybe they were attracted by the smell of a delicious dwarf!" (She then added sotto voce that perhaps goblins didn't mind parasites—her half whisper cut through the air like a shot.)

"GRGB?!"

The goblin tumbled from the lead warg, slamming into the ground, everything above his neck blown away. From the way the animals behind split left and right, leaping over his body, maybe the goblins really did have control of their mounts. Then again, even the now-riderless warg continued straight ahead, unperturbed by the loss of its rider.

"WARRG?!"

High Elf Archer's second volley finished it off. She drew more bud-tipped arrows from her quiver. "I wish these riders were a little stupider..."

"How many are there?" Goblin Slayer asked from inside the wagon, gazing out over the field.

"Maybe ten of them, from what I can see. But I think there might be more in the distance!" came the answer from up top.

Goblin Slayer grunted softly. He hated open spaces. Confined areas were so much easier.

"Um, here you go…!" Priestess said, fetching his short bow and a quiver from the baggage. She didn't know how to shoot—she'd learned slinging, but it would be difficult from a moving vehicle. Instead, she busied herself making sure Goblin Slayer was armed.

"That helps," he said, giving the bowstring a quick tug to check the fit, then nocking an arrow into the bow and pulling it back. It made a noisy, unpleasant *creak*, nothing like the musical twanging of High Elf Archer's shots.

His arrow flew over the field in a low arc, piercing the foreleg of one of the wargs with a *thock*.

"WGGR?!"

The creature yelped and threw its rider. At this speed, knowing how to land safely from a fall wouldn't help much—and goblins didn't know how to do that in the first place. The monster landed headfirst, bounced a few times, and stopped moving, dead.

"That's one, for starters."

"Hey, not a bad shot," High Elf Archer commented, peeking into the wagon (upside down). "I didn't know you could use a bow."

"Not as well as you."

"Well, naturally!"

The elf was bursting with confidence. She disappeared back above the wagon, her braid bouncing behind her like a tail. Priestess looked up, but there wasn't so much as a dimple in the wagon cover; her much older friend hardly even seemed to be there. Such was the athleticism of the high elves—humans couldn't hope to match them.

"Hey, help me down," Baturu now said. She was crouched in the cramped luggage area, trying to find a way to stand up.

"Help you down?" Priestess repeated, starting to her feet. "You want to fight?!"

"Of course I do!"

As if in answer to Baturu's shout (though of course not really), a hand spear came whooshing at the wagon—although it was a crude product and a poor throw, not even managing to lodge in the wood.

"GROOGB! GORRRBBG!"

"WARGGW!!"

A pack horse harnessed to a wagon couldn't hope to match the pace of a warg. The goblins, convinced that they had made up the gap by their own skill, cheered and threw spears at the wagon. Most of them barely reached the vehicle, and those that did mostly bounced off it. But a spare few tore through the cover, their rough-hewn tips savaging the cargo.

Still…

Never overconfident, never letting her guard down, Priestess took a deep breath and assessed the situation calmly. "Even if they catch us, we should be able to handle them!"

"They'd never beat us, but I'd hate to let them think they've got us on the run!" Baturu said. Her attitude was as sharp and true as a blade.

Priestess cast an uncertain glance around the inside of the wagon. Goblin Slayer was mumbling, "Two…three," as he killed goblins, driving back the party's pursuers. High Elf Archer was about the same business. Lizard Priest was working the reins, urging the horse to go ever faster.

It was Dwarf Shaman whose eyes she finally met. He was enough of an old hand to know that the spell caster had nothing to do at this moment. Instead, he looked at Priestess and Baturu as if to ask whether they had something interesting for him. "Really think you can do it?" he asked.

"A toothless dog does not howl," Baturu replied with the sharpness of someone who thought she'd been insulted. In Priestess's eyes, her small body (well, the small *human* part of her body) seemed to be pulsing with life. A fireball just before it flew, embers glowing in the hearth: For some reason, that's what Priestess saw.

Dwarf Shaman ran a hand through his white beard, then called to his party leader, who was busy firing arrows out from under the cover of the wagon. "I think it's time to let the young lady show us what she can do."

"Hrm..." Goblin Slayer grunted softly, meanwhile unleashing yet another volley. It couldn't be easy to mentally calculate where both a moving wagon and moving wargs would be relative to each other a few seconds in the future: The little arrow pierced a warg's foot without ever slowing it down.

Goblin Slayer sighed. "How does it look to you?"

"I doubt there are many who can match a centaur on the open plain!" Lizard Priest replied in a howl from the driver's seat, where he held the party's fate literally in his hands. It must have nettled him not to be able to be part of the fight himself, yet still the thrill of battle coursed through his veins. He showed himself to be a very rational lizardman, however, for despite his excitement, he resisted treating the wagon like a chariot. "They do say one must test a horse to know its quality..."

"Very well," Goblin Slayer said. At that moment, he had no idea whether it was the right choice or not. And it was pointless to know you had made the right choice only later. He nodded. "I'll cover you."

"Excellent!" Baturu exclaimed and drew her katana, leaping atop the luggage rack.

Priestess hurried over, preparing to help tighten the clasps of her armor, which she had loosened. "I'll help you...!"

"My thanks!"

Priestess didn't recognize the armor, which came from the plain and, more, belonged to a centaur. But it was still just armor. She could figure out how to close a clasp.

She'd seen the others handling their equipment as long as she had been a part of this party; she was more than capable of helping here. She hustled from one side of Baturu to the other, and meanwhile the fight went on.

"I assume you heard that," Goblin Slayer called over his head. "Can you work with us?"

"Make it an order, not a question!" High Elf Archer shot back.

No problem, then. Goblin Slayer drew back his bow and let loose at the nearest goblin.

"GORGB?!"

"WAGGG?!"

At the same time, a bud-tipped arrow came down and pierced the now-riderless warg through the jaw from top to bottom. The creature's corpse went tumbling, forcing the riders behind to swerve to avoid it.

An opening.

"Ready!" Priestess called. Baturu rose to her feet. Lizard Priest registered all this from his place up front.

"Shall I reduce our speed, then?" he asked.

"Drive like the wind, Master Lizard!" Baturu cried, all but dropping backward out of the wagon and hitting the ground running. It was incredible; she lost no speed at all and was already going full tilt when her hooves met the earth.

Just one step. That was all it took for her to be a body's length ahead of the enemy, as if charting the squares as she went.

"Ha! *Ha!*" Her laughter cut through the wind, which caught her hair and tail, causing them to billow out behind her like proud war banners. The muscles of her equine body worked visibly, tearing up the ground, carrying her along as though on an ocean of grass.

She was like a blue gale, a streak of cerulean light tearing across the green of the field. Priestess couldn't look away from her. This wasn't how she had seemed when she was asserting herself in the Adventurers Guild or when she had been chatting on the wagon. Then she'd seemed alive but not alive. She wasn't where she *belonged.*

Who knew that someone could be so beautiful, born to the one purpose of running through the fields? Priestess had never known before. Even Dwarf Shaman stopped drinking his wine, and High Elf Archer let her hand slacken on her bow.

As for Goblin Slayer…who could be sure?

"GOROOGB!"

"GBBGBR! GRROGBRRG!!"

The goblins, naturally, had no appreciation of such things. In their eyes, the centaur was simply foolish prey who had jumped down right into their clutches.

A woman! A girl! Big. Highly edible. Good to play *with. Fine equipment. What a waste.*

Skin her! Break her legs. How she'll scream! How she'll cry! What fun it will be!

You back off—I will do it! Don't be stupid; she's mine. Mine. Mine. Mine! Mine!

Goblins think only about themselves. They always assume it is they who will get whatever it is they want. Thus the first goblin didn't *think* as he charged ahead at his quarry. The second goblin, oh so smart (or so he thought himself), held back, mocking his companion for an idiot.

It saved his life.

"Hrrraaah!"

A single swipe of the sword, Baturu's great katana kicking up a gale in the process. She was like the swordsman of elven legend, her slash a silver beam that seemed like it could cut all the grass in the four corners in a single stroke. So sharp it was almost audible, it knocked the goblin in the van off his mount.

"GROGB?!"

"WGRG?!?!"

The warg's head went flying, and the goblin's hideous face was cloven in two. What must the "smart" goblin have thought as he saw his companion turn into a fountain of dark blood?

Whatever he might have thought he would do next, he would never get a chance to do it.

"Yaaaaah!"

The second strike came with a step in that seemed impossible from "horseback." From shoulder level, the sword hewed the goblin in half diagonally like a piece of firewood.

"GBBBRORGB?!?!"

"Hah! Yah!"

To the right, to the left: Blood flew in a tempest as Baturu laughed. And all the while, arrows came from the wagon, whittling down the goblins' numbers—this battle was as good as over. Each time the centaur made her blade howl, the goblins—and their wargs—took fright. But fright afforded them no escape.

"......"

For a very long time, Priestess didn't blink; taking in the sight, she almost forgot to breathe. Without a horse's head in front of her to get in the way, Baturu was able to fight vastly more effectively than a mounted human—not that Priestess, unschooled in tactics, could know how to do that. It wouldn't have mattered if she had.

Priestess understood only this: There were a great many more able fighters than Baturu in the Four-Cornered World. Heavy Warrior with his greatsword. Spearman with his polearm. Even the *goði* of the north and his lightning-clad blade. And for sheer destructive power, there was the secret technique she had seen, just once, from Female Knight. No doubt any experienced warrior watching Baturu fight would have seen how much growing she still had to do.

Yet they were dealing with goblins. The weakest monsters in the Four-Cornered World.

Priestess, who had been on many goblin hunts now, would never have trumpeted her accomplishments in those endeavors. To roll up the sleeves of your crude garment and overpower some goblins was nothing to be proud of.

And yet, even so, she still found it beautiful.

"That looks like it," Baturu said a moment later, shaking the blood from her blade and sheathing it in its scabbard.

Her breath came hard; her face was flushed, and sweat glistened on her cheeks. She didn't even glance at the bodies littering the ground as she trotted back to the wagon. She got her legs up onto the luggage rack, trying to board the vehicle even as it continued to roll.

"I'll help you!" Priestess said, reaching out.

"Hrm..." Baturu looked somewhat uncertain, glancing between her own large hand and Priestess's, which was more delicate but certainly not merely pretty. Then she slowly, hesitantly clasped it, though her expression remained indeterminate. "Thanks..."

"Not at all!" Priestess said and tugged with a "hup," though with her strength, it was hard to say how much help she actually was. Not much, perhaps—but it was important.

"...That was impressive," Goblin Slayer noted, unconcerned with the specifics.

Priestess offered a waterskin to Baturu, who took it, again hesitantly, and began drinking. Goblin Slayer watched them as he put away his bow and arrows.

"Here, have a drink," Priestess offered, coming over to him and offering him the canteen.

"Mm." Goblin Slayer took it gratefully, throwing a slug of water through the slats of his visor. After a battle like that, even lukewarm water cut with wine was indescribably satisfying.

"Not that I wish to belittle your achievements..." Baturu, who must have been feeling the same way about the water, finally let out a breath, scratching her cheek shyly. "But feats of arms against goblins are nothing to crow about."

"I agree completely," Goblin Slayer said with utmost seriousness, his helmet bobbing up and down. One ought not to think in terms of success when it came to dealing with goblins, nor had he ever done so.

Was that simply a wandering tribe? he thought. He stared after the bodies, which had already vanished. Should he stop the carriage, go back, and check? *No.* Time was of the essence now. He had to prioritize the investigation in the water town. That was his decision. *If there is even the slightest possibility that goblins are involved...*

Of course, even Goblin Slayer realized that this was a pathological obsession—yet he also knew that, at the same time, it was something he had to keep in his heart.

"'Oh! I'm not smart enough to be skeptical!' he says. That's not decency, it's idiocy!" he remembered his master saying as he grinned amid the blowing snow. *"The guy who realizes it might be dangerous and runs away is the smart guy—the one who decides he doesn't care is the adventurer!"*

Goblin Slayer couldn't claim to fully understand this. Indeed, how much of what he'd been taught *could* he claim to understand? Still, he was resolved to use what few wits and little skill he did have to do what he had to do.

Do or do not. That was all there was—and that, he had learned a very long time ago.

"We'll hurry to the water town," Goblin Slayer said. "We should also switch driver and lookout duties."

"You got it," replied Dwarf Shaman, heaving his portly frame up and heading for the driver's bench. "Hey, Scaly," he called, tapping Lizard Priest on the shoulder; he managed to nimbly swaps places with the huge lizardman. Dwarf Shaman might have taken a little sip of fire wine, but the God of Wine would look the other way for a drinking dwarf.

Now Dwarf Shaman said, "I'd heard rumors about the centaur troops, but that was something to see."

"I only regret that I did not see it at all, driving as I was," Lizard Priest said, squeezing himself under the cover of the wagon. He didn't sound too terribly regretful, though. He curled his tail to avoid getting in Goblin Slayer's way as he went by; then he let out a breath, swiveled his great long neck, and rolled his eyes merrily. "Would it be too upsetting if I said I hope to have a chance to see your work with the bow someday?"

"Not that I'm angry about it," said High Elf Archer, who was lying easily atop the wagon, "but it looks like it's gonna be goblins again this time..."

There was no sense that anything, be it spear or sword or fiery stone, was going to fall through the clear blue sky at that moment. It was mere days later that she would sigh to herself, realizing how right she had been.

INTERLUDE

One Mustn't Lose to a Worthy Opponent

"Think they've reached the water town by now?"

"Maybe..."

They were at the tavern at the Adventurers Guild. It was too late to be "morning" but too early to be "afternoon." Guild Girl and Cow Girl were sharing a late breakfast at a round table and talking about a subject they had in common—news of *him*.

Breakfast? Why not, once in a while? It was a whim pursued with some vigor.

"...On an adventure, by definition, you don't know what's going to happen," Guild Girl said with an elegant smile. So who knew—they might still be on the road or out on the open field.

Amazing...

That was how Cow Girl always felt about that smile.

Guild Girl had a balanced figure with its lovely silhouette, the neatly combed hair. The faint aroma of perfume. When Cow Girl compared that with herself, still basically in her work clothes, she couldn't help thinking—

No! It's not a contest, she told herself. She couldn't seem to stop from believing, though, that girls from good families sure were lucky.

"It's not as great as you're thinking," Guild Girl said, as if, on top of everything else, she could read Cow Girl's mind.

She'd said she'd been busy all morning, although she didn't *look* like someone who'd been so busy that she hadn't been able to stop for breakfast. She looked effortlessly stylish, like she had breeziness to spare. It couldn't have been easy to keep up an appearance like that.

"I know it's not," Cow Girl said, "but I can't help being impressed..."

"I could say the very same thing to you!"

Spending all morning sweating and laboring on a farm! Guild Girl felt she could never do such a thing.

The two of them looked at each other and giggled—the grass really was always greener on the other side!

"But, I mean... Setting aside that issue..." Cow Girl gestured with her spoon, drawing a circle in the air (not very ladylike). "You've been to balls and stuff, right? In fancy dresses?"

"Hmm, I suppose I have. Purely for social reasons."

"So it's like the assemblies my uncle goes to..."

Well, those never sounded like much fun. Cow Girl imagined the balls Guild Girl had attended as basically one of those, if dancing broke out.

"You go around trying to remember who's who and how they act and forcing yourself to be polite to everyone."

"Sounds rough."

"Yes, well, unfortunately those connections are how work gets done, so you can't beg off all the time."

In politics and in business, it was difficult to do anything without some sort of bond with the people you were trying to work with—and nobles made it their business to make things happen in the nation.

So there you had it. Guild Girl's pretty chest rose proudly. "I got myself out of all that as soon as I could—by becoming an employee of the Adventurers Guild!"

"Ha-ha-ha. Yeah, I definitely think all that's pretty amazing."

For one thing, Cow Girl had never had the courage to go rushing off on her own. She questioned whether she would have it now. It wasn't that she wanted to become an adventurer—she wanted to be a princess. She had ever since she was little.

From that perspective, at least...

"...*Rescue the princess*, huh?" she murmured.

"A classic adventure," Guild Girl said with a smile.

I guess I'm a little…jealous. Of Guild Girl with her smile and of the centaur princess whose name and face she didn't know. It was just a distant, hovering cloud in her heart, but it didn't feel very good.

A "hmm" escaped Guild Girl. It sounded so much like *him* that Cow Girl looked up in spite of herself. "It's just an ordinary thing. I was thinking of selling it…," Guild Girl said.

"What? What?" Cow Girl urged.

"There's a jousting tournament in the capital and, well, I've got an invitation."

"You, uh, you do?" Cow Girl looked into the middle distance, thinking. She didn't really know the word *jousting,* but she had a faint recognition of it. *Oh yeah. When we were really little, he said…* "Is that that thing where knights go all *ba-ba-ba-ba!* and then *thoom*? That's it, isn't it?"

"Well, that's not *all* there is to it… But I guess you've got the gist."

Cow Girl was glad she'd remembered accurately what he'd said. Although she had no idea if it would be remotely interesting to watch.

That was when Guild Girl said something completely unexpected: "If you'd like, how about we go together?"

"Whaaa…?"

Cow Girl blinked and looked at her friend. She didn't look like she was teasing. This invitation was in earnest. Cow Girl opened her mouth to answer, but the words wouldn't come out. In the end, she couldn't muster a response. Didn't say she wanted to go, didn't say she didn't want to go. And a dress! What would she do about a— Well, no, wait, she had one of those. Basically. Ummm. Ummmm…

"Anyway, just think about it," Guild Girl said.

"…Mn," Cow Girl finally managed with a nod.

Guild Girl drank the last of her tea, then set down her cup without so much as a *clink* and rose from her chair. "I guess I'd better get back to work," she said.

"Er, uh," Cow Girl started, nodding and watching her. "Have a good day?"

Sure. Guild Girl smiled—elegant indeed. Cow Girl watched the braid bounce on her back as she went. She kicked her feet, unable to say anything.

It was a strange time of day. The tavern was quiet, and there was no one else—well, not quite. There was one other customer, a small—er, *lean* girl with black hair who looked deep in thought. There were several slices of cheap black bread on her plate, and she was munching on them assiduously, almost ravenously. She looked like the kind who would peck at her food, yet her eyes showed a desperation to eat more.

Some brand-new equipment, with just a few small scratches on it, was propped on the chair, and around her neck was a status tag.

"Guess you're an adventurer?" Cow Girl offered.

"......?" The girl peeked up from her plate, wiping the crumbs of bread from her mouth and looking quickly from one side to the other before she located Cow Girl. "Oh!" she almost squeaked. "Y-y-yes, I am." She nodded, looking equal parts shy and happy.

Wow, she's adorable, Cow Girl thought. A young girl who was eager, serious, and seemed to be rushing forward. So different from herself.

"Going on an adventure after this?"

"Oh, um, well..." The girl was almost pitifully lost for words before she produced an answer that didn't quite seem like an answer: "I'm, uh, trying my best!"

"That's a great plan. Best of luck!" Cow Girl said with a wave, and a smile like a flower blossomed on the black-haired girl's face. She nodded vigorously before shoving the rest of the bread into her mouth. She washed it down with some water, coughing, then rushed out of the building, not neglecting to bow to Padfoot Waitress, who was sweeping near the entrance. Her backpack bounced as she went, and at her chest was a charm, a black onyx.

Cow Girl watched her idly. "An adventure... Huh."

The truth was, she didn't know if they were any fun. But they certainly seemed to have *his* attention.

Noboru Kannatuki

CHAPTER 3
FIND SILVER BLAZE!

"Would you like us to tend to your hooves? We have horseshoes if you'd like."

"Th-this is most embarrassing…!"

At the great Temple of Law in the water town, Goblin Slayer and his party were received most hospitably. Even though it was evening when they arrived, the clerics welcomed them cordially, leaving Priestess unsure how to express her appreciation. What made her heart really skip a beat, though, was the temple's bath. It was bigger than any bath one could have hoped for in a temple on the frontier. A large, beautiful space, full of warm steam. Priestess found it endlessly wonderful.

Just like Lady Archbishop.

That archbishop, who was there in the bath now. When Priestess thought back on the last time they'd been in here together, she felt her body grow warm.

She couldn't think of a bath larger than this one except perhaps the Great Bath in the capital, which had its own spring supplying hot water.

In any case…

"It's fine. It's great! Sure, it's a little surprising at first, but it's just like regular bathing," High Elf Archer insisted.

"You would wash your body in front of other people? There's something wrong with you…," Baturu said. They were in the changing room, and she was acting in a way that made Priestess think of High Elf Archer back when they'd just met.

The temple official who'd made the suggestion about the horseshoes didn't seem fazed by the centaur; maybe she was used to dealing with people of all walks of life. Their timing must have been good, for they didn't see any other clerics' vestments in the changing area.

So it won't bother anyone if our group is a little lively!

Priestess folded her clothes carefully, wrapping her mail in some cloth, and nodded to herself. High Elf Archer noticed and smiled ruefully. Baturu gave them both a questioning look, but it was a small thing.

"Do you not take baths in the plain country?" Priestess asked.

"...Wiping down our bodies is enough to suffice," Baturu said.

This land of wind and dry grass and open fields—in Priestess's mind, it somehow made her think of the desert she'd visited.

"Anyway," Baturu went on, her face flushing and her tail waving broadly, "who would ever let someone else touch their hooves? Do humans *do* that sort of thing?"

"Sounds a bit like our ears," High Elf Archer said, flicking hers demonstratively.

"Our ears and tails are also off-limits," Baturu added, her own ears lying back on her head.

To be fair, I was a little shy about letting people see my ankles back when we made the sacred wine...

Priestess looked from one of them to the other, tapped a thoughtful finger to her lips, and then nodded. "Well, let's go ahead and get in!"

"Seconded!" High Elf Archer said.

"Wh-what do you two think you're doing?" Baturu asked.

It ended up as a bit of a quarrel. Not a real fight—if Baturu had been moved to bring her powerful kicks into the equation, things would have been over quickly. The fact that she didn't meant she was either being considerate or holding back on them.

Either way, I'm just as glad, Priestess thought.

Between them, with many a smile and "c'mon, now," she and High Elf Archer managed to coax Baturu to strip down. She had golden skin, tanned by the sun, and the muscles of her arms and legs were

toned and firm. She wasn't bulky, but she nonetheless looked different from the willowy Priestess or the statuesque High Elf Archer. Her body, shaped by and for running across the plain, had a functional beauty; it would have been a shame, in its own way, to hide it under bathwear. Of course, that would only hide the top half of her—the bottom half was still a gorgeous equine body…

You know, I wonder…

Were centaur women the same *down there* as human women? Priestess blushed at her own crude thought.

"Hnnngh… I've never been so embarrassed…," Baturu said, her hooves clopping on the marble.

High Elf Archer grinned like a cat. "Just think of it as cultural exchange!" She was very much fond of bathing these days, and she quickly stretched out her legs and relaxed. It was a gesture unbecoming a princess of the elves, yet strangely, it was still beautiful, so lovely it could have been a painting.

Priestess kept stealing glances at High Elf Archer out of the corner of her eye as she placed a cloth (not the one for her mail) on the floor. "Would this work?" she asked.

"Yeah… Sorry."

"Not at all," Priestess said.

Baturu slowly bent down and laid on the cloth. Priestess lowered her little butt down next to the centaur, and all three of them let out contented sighs.

They might quibble and quarrel, but the warm air relaxed them from the cores of their bodies, releasing the tension in their muscles. It was tiring, rattling along in a wagon for so long. The sweat that rolled off their bodies, flushed from the steam, seemed to take the day's fatigue with it. As they relaxed into it, it made their hearts lighter. The heart and the body are inseparable, after all, so it's hard to affect one without affecting the other.

Hence why Baturu's voice was languorous as she asked, "But why a bath, though…?"

"It's important to rest your body after a long trip," Priestess said, sounding equally relaxed, and she added, "Besides, you always get to be better friends by sharing a tub." That was just something she'd discovered through experience—that the easiest times to talk were just before you fell asleep or in the bath—in any case, when everything and everyone was jumbled together, that was the perfect time.

"What do you think?" High Elf Archer asked, her eyes half-closed. "Starting to trust us now?"

"Truth be told, not quite," Baturu said.

Which is another way of saying she trusts us enough to tell us she doesn't trust us! Priestess thought, and it brought a smile to her face, even though Baturu still looked put out.

The centaur stared at Priestess dubiously and continued. "Aren't adventurers just uncouth ruffians anyway?"

"Uncouth ruffians with the state's seal of approval," High Elf Archer quipped.

"But *we* are not subjects of your king," Baturu said, her tone still sharp.

The high elf—also not a subject of the king—smiled and shrugged; Priestess, for her part, let the comment roll right off her back. Understanding each other didn't mean always saying, *Oh yes! You're absolutely right!* If it did, how could a lizardman, a dwarf, an elf, and some humans all go hunting goblins together?

"I guess you must not have liked the idea of your princess becoming an adventurer," Priestess suggested.

"It…it was her own honorable decision. It's not mine to comment on," Baturu said—which basically meant *no.* The centaur pressed a washcloth to her face, pretending to wipe away some sweat from her glowing cheeks, and rubbed vigorously. "The only reason I came along with you was to make sure you actually did the job—and didn't just say you were *still looking* while you wasted my time and my money." She stared at them, her expression hard, tense. "I can imagine some cunning operator trying to pull just such a scheme."

"Eh, lots of humans can't tell the difference between clever and sneaky," High Elf Archer said.

Priestess felt a little bit attacked. But how could a centaur or a high elf be expected to follow the human laws of a human kingdom set by a human king? It was hard enough even for other humans.

Read the whole history of the Four-Cornered World and you would never find an ideal place with no problems. Thus, that wasn't an issue Priestess could address. Instead, she looked up at the statue of the hermaphroditic Deity of the Basin and that of the Supreme God above it. This wasn't quite a matter of Law or Order, but…it shared the same roots. There was no simple answer—which was precisely why the gods had entrusted it to Pray-ers.

"But it might be true—that we never find her," High Elf Archer said, drawing Priestess back into the present moment. She made an idle circle in the air with her finger until her digit came to rest by her cheek; her face was tinged with some frustration. "Human money doesn't grow on trees, you know."

"Doesn't that go without saying?" Baturu mumbled, bringing an unexpected smile to Priestess's face. The cleric tried to apologize to her friend, who was giving her an *oh what* look, but she couldn't stop giggling.

"But even so," Priestess said proudly, even though it was all she could do to wipe the tears from her eyes, "we won't stop looking until we find her. That's what adventurers do."

"Yeah!" High Elf Archer said, puffing out her modest chest. "That's right!"

"Eep!" Priestess exclaimed when she found herself suddenly confronted with the magically delicate body, and the two of them soon fell to jabbering. Only Baturu remained resolutely, sullenly silent.

§

"My goodness… To think you would show up so suddenly. I would have liked to make some preparations."

"I see."

Goblin Slayer had been shown into one of the innermost chambers of the Temple of Law. The last golden rays of the day's sunlight poured down amid the chalk pillars, carving bright streaks in the purple tendrils of night. In the garden, a white sacred beast lay in repose, a bird perched on its scales. You could listen closely, but all you would hear would be the trembling of the grass and flowers in the wind and the burbling of water.

It was a calm, quiet environment where serenity reigned.

The woman who was the master of this place, her body covered in soft flesh, bent over, forming alluring curves. A pale thigh peeked out from under her thin vestments, looking as delicate and beautiful as glass. She proved that there were women in this world so beautiful, they could capture a person's heart just sitting there. A succubus looking for a form in which to incarnate herself could find no better example.

Not that many succubi would wish to imitate this woman if they knew the deeds she had done.

Sword Maiden furrowed her brow and pursed her lips at the man standing before her as if she was the most innocent of girls. "It puts me in quite a pickle."

"I see." Goblin Slayer nodded brusquely, then accepted her invitation to sit down across from her. He knew this was a personal space belonging to Sword Maiden, the archbishop who shouldered the burden of Order in this area; he had been here before. It had always been a purified place, but today that fact was underlined by its tidiness.

The cleric withdrew to the entryway of the room with a bow; Sword Maiden acknowledged her with a nod. Then she put her hand to her ample bosom as if to still the pounding of her heart. "Might I ask what brings you here today?"

"Several things," Goblin Slayer answered, still businesslike. "But first, goblins."

"Goodness..." Sword Maiden sounded like a young woman hearing some horrible tale. She put a hand to her rosy cheeks, and maybe her eyes under her bandage had gone wide with fear.

Goblin Slayer knew the reaction was heartfelt. Thus he chose his words carefully—but he made no attempt to hide anything. "On our way here, we were attacked by goblins. They had...wargs, or whatever they're called. Mounted troops."

"A wandering tribe, do you suppose?"

"I can't be certain." There had been no time to investigate—or rather, he had prioritized getting here (he dutifully corrected his own understanding of his actions). Then he asked, just to be sure: "Have goblins been appearing around here again?"

"Not at all!" Sword Maiden exclaimed, her voice going up a register. The only ones who had heard her sound like that were the cleric who attended upon her personally, the other four members of Goblin Slayer's party—and Goblin Slayer himself.

Sword Maiden looked at the ground as if embarrassed to have let herself be heard that way. A ripple passed through her golden hair as she shook her head. "No... There's been nothing of the sort," she said much more quietly, and then she looked up as if to gauge his reaction. She seemed to be peering through the visor of his metal helmet, looking beseechingly at him. To her eyes, neither the night darkness nor the shadows made a whit of difference. "There's been no sign of goblins in this city since you got rid of them for us."

"Hrm..."

"There have been evil elements, of course. But with that much, we can..."

...make do.

It was not a statement of pride—with her position and her power, it was simple fact.

The forces of Chaos would be rampant in any city as large as the water town. Agents of dark cults hid in dark places, demons corrupted people's hearts, and unsavory nobles worked their own sort of mischief.

Vice was everywhere, be it in the lawless wilderness or the civilized settlement; it simply took a different form in each. How could one both praise the bravery of those who fought against these forces and simultaneously deride them as incompetent?

Goblin Slayer was aware that he knew nothing. It must be so difficult simply to stand alone, believing in the gods, forcing down one's fear of goblins. The woman before him had accomplished things he could not dream of doing.

"Whatever the case," he said, "if it's not goblins, then it is beyond me."

"Yes," Sword Maiden replied, grasping the sword and scales. "Thankfully...and most unfortunately." Then a mournful whisper escaped her lips. "You will not have to trouble yourself."

"I don't know if it's related to the matter I'm pursuing, but it is a fact that goblins appeared," he told her.

"I'll take extra caution. If they're in some vanguard of Chaos, they might be a sign of a shadow about to fall on the town."

One thing above all others: Goblins ought to be destroyed. On that point, this man and woman agreed absolutely. They nodded at each other. Although only Sword Maiden flinched at the way her cleric-attendant privately sighed to herself.

"Well," Sword Maiden began reluctantly, afraid to voice such an untoward question, "if you're going to be here for very long, you must need a place to stay..." She then mumbled, "If it's no trouble..." Her pale fingers fidgeted with the hem of her dress. The same hem goblins had torn at. It was still beautiful, like her eyes. "...Perhaps, if you've no objection, you would like to stay at this temple."

"That would be a help," Goblin Slayer said, nodding earnestly under his helmet. He was truly fortunate to receive the help of others. "I know it's quite an imposition, but if we could turn to you for this, I would be grateful."

"Goodness...!" This time, she sounded like a young noblewoman receiving a poem from a man she adored. "If there's anything I can do, anything at all, please don't hesitate to tell me." She dipped her head, blushing so furiously that she was embarrassed to even take a step forward.

"I am looking for someone. I'm on"—here he paused and hesitated for a long moment—"an adventure."

"You're looking for someone?" Sword Maiden murmured, the words dropping into the twilight space between them. The cleric moved soundlessly, lighting a candle in a candleholder. The flickering flame mingled with the last wisps of the sinking sun and set the shadows dancing.

Was this what they called an air of mystery? To Goblin Slayer's rustic sensibilities, it seemed so—not that he really knew what an "air of mystery" was supposed to constitute.

"We went on many adventures but rarely a search... Er, never mind." Sword Maiden giggled as if recalling some game she'd played as a child. "I suppose we did. Down in the Dungeon."

"Unfortunately, I suspect this will take place in town. If the object of our search is still here."

©Noboru Kannatuki

"And who are you looking for exactly...?"

"A centaur," Goblin Slayer said. "A princess of her people, I'm told. Beautiful, with a lock of hair that falls over her forehead like a shooting star."

"..."

Sword Maiden found herself unable to answer immediately. She was gazing at the night that lay over the garden. The gloomy hour had come on so suddenly.

Could the stars and the twin moons be seen this night? Surely not. The air felt too damp for that.

After a long moment, she approached him gingerly. "I would be lying if I said I didn't have a guess. Although I know not if it will help you..."

"I don't mind," Goblin Slayer replied decisively. "I must investigate everything, one thing at a time."

"Yes, that's just how you are..." He had been back *then*, too. Her lips softened into a smile as if she was sharing a secret. "Are you familiar with Silver Blaze?"

§

A dust cloud puffed up as someone kicked off—*smack!*—under the blue sky. There was a colorful flash, colorful figures, charging forward so quickly they were almost a blur.

The shrine maidens!

Red, blue, green, yellow, brown, black: The beautiful maidens were dressed in scintillating vestments of every color. Perhaps in imitation of the Trade God, the god of the wind, or maybe the Valkyrie, goddess of victory. They raced forward in line astern, these women so dear and so beautiful one could fall in love with them at first glimpse.

Those lower limbs that kicked off the earth, propelling them forward, were not human but equine. They were centaur women, running along the ground with their legs like wings.

The spectators packed into the coliseum let out a collective sound of amazement. The racecourse began wide enough for all six to run abreast, but after one or two turns, two of them side by side was the most they could manage.

The maidens pressed and pushed, shoulder to shoulder, vying to forge ahead or falling back to conserve their strength.

Out front was a delicate young lady, some of the hair on the side of her head parted toward the back. She had run at the front since the moment the race started, though it was impossible to say where in that small frame she kept such power and strength. Her performance seemed to say: If one could run flat out from the beginning to the end, then victory was guaranteed. But nothing is guaranteed.

Hot on her heels was a white—no, dappled—young woman, running easily. If the lady in front was running flat out, this girl seemed to have speed in reserve. That made her smile all the more overpowering—a smile that said she enjoyed nothing more than slicing through the wind like this. This dappled young woman, it was plain to see, was the star of this show.

Through turn two, turn three, the two of them battled, picking up speed, threatening to pull away—but there was someone behind them who refused to let them do so. A young woman with a yellow rose in her hair pressed forward, gritting her teeth. If the contest ahead was between the flat-out and the relaxed, perhaps we could say she represented pure determination.

Her otherwise cute outfit was spattered with mud, but she didn't care; it seemed like her lungs might explode, yet she paid them no mind. It was not natural talent or lineage that supported this girl as she bore down on the front runners but sheer, unvarnished effort. Her arms worked furiously, her hooves veritably dragged her forward; she went onward, ever onward, thinking only of victory.

They rounded the final turn, and all that remained was the last straight. Whoever could pull ahead at this moment would receive the winner's laurels.

Suddenly, there was a thunderclap from behind. A centaur in men's clothing, a rather tall centaur at that, who had been holding station at the back of the field was suddenly making a move. Each time her hooves hit the ground, dirt flew everywhere and there was an audible crash.

One step, two steps, three steps—every stride ate up the distance as she closed in on the women ahead. In the blink of an eye, it was a four-horse race.

Traveling like a bolt of lightning, the woman in dark clothes spared a momentary smile for her worthy opponents. The noble-looking lady tried to ignore her. The dappled girl gave her a smile back. The girl with the yellow rose in her hair continued to push forward.

Each time someone pulled out in front, someone else would close in on them. They ran side by side, jostling each other, trying to gain that one step that would put them ahead. Who would win? Even the gods couldn't know. The die had been cast.

It was impossible to blink; there was no time even to breathe. Every eye in the arena was fixed on the contest. Everything in the oval arena at that moment was for them, these young ladies, the aurigae.

And finally…

"*Ave Caesar!* Long live the king!" cried the winner, her voice resounding up to the spectators, who responded with cheering, showering her with glory.

§

"The king! Is he here?" Priestess asked.

"Naw. It's just a tradition," Dwarf Shaman said easily as confetti flew into the blue sky. He had grilled cat meat in one hand and a cup of wine in the other. Gambling he didn't touch, but he still seemed to be living his best life.

He was a stark contrast to Priestess, who couldn't get over the excitement of her first race. "Amazing!" was all she could find to say at first, until her question about the king finally made its way out. *Ave Caesar*, she heard, yet when she looked at the nobles' seats, she saw no sign of the royal presence. It was understandably confusing to those not in the know.

They were at an oval coliseum; Priestess had heard there was a place like this in the water town, but this was her first visit. The structure was made of heavy stone, with seats that went up story after story, and almost all of them were filled today. Priestess had never seen so many people in one place, to say nothing of such excitement. She'd heard tell, of course, of how crowds thrilled at the centaurs' races, but…

It's still just…amazing!

©Noboru Kannatuki

She found herself rising off the soft rush mat under her behind more often than she sat on it—and they said the Circus Maximus in the royal capital was even grander than this! She could hardly imagine what would happen if a girl raised in the countryside like her was to go there.

"Unless I'm very much mistaken, those races started with war chariots—and I think the greeting was given in the middle of the race!" Dwarf Shaman said.

"The centaur races have been rather popular lately," said a grinning young woman—the one who had invited the party here. She looked pleased to be there with them, and indeed, she had once been a member of their group. Now she was a prosperous businessperson—it was Female Merchant. They hadn't seen her since their adventure in the desert.

She had been quick to accept Sword Maiden's request—how could she object to taking these dear friends of hers to see all the excitement at the coliseum?

"Both the Quadriga and the Biga," Female Merchant told the group. "The salutation is the most recent form of a tradition that's changed over time, once including songs and dances."

"You humans get so attached to your traditions—but then you change them at the drop of a hat. I don't understand it," High Elf Archer said, although she was happily clutching a handful of gambling tickets. The fact that she didn't throw them away suggested that either she had successfully picked a winner or she didn't grasp what they were for.

Then again, maybe it was the trendy (in the water town) clothing she and Female Merchant had plotted to wear (giggling all the while). To Priestess, the outfits seemed to show an embarrassing amount of skin.

I can't quite bring myself to look at them, she thought, rather in spite of herself—though at the same time, the outfits looked like they would be nice and cool in this hot weather. If nothing else, it certainly showed off the high elf's healthy body to best effect—which is to say, it looked very good on her. *Maybe I should've asked for one, too*, Priestess thought—just for a second—but she quickly reproved herself, reminding herself that it wasn't good to waste money.

High Elf Archer, for her part, seemed to be having too good of a time to worry about her clothes—maybe she was caught up in the excitement of the crowd.

"That outfit is quite becoming on you," Lizard Priest commented, nodding his long head somberly, then taking a bite of the cat meat in his hand.

"Oh, thanks," High Elf Archer said, waving at him with a feline grin.

Lizard Priest swallowed—he seemed to find the food quite tasty. "I'm most intrigued by the idea of a contest between battle chariots," he said, then mumbled, "And how much better it would be if there was cheese!" which brought a giggle from his high elf companion.

"I'm always surprised to remember that you do like to take the reins, don't you?" she said.

"Yes, I'm inspired by one particular saga that tells the story of a man who fights false charges of being an assassin by means of a chariot race against his mortal enemy."

"That's not even the main *point* of that saga," High Elf Archer added with a wry smile. "Besides, that's a really long one!"

"Never heard of an elf complainin' about anything being too long before!" Dwarf Shaman remarked.

"Anyway, I'm glad we saw this. They're really fast, those centaurs." High Elf Archer was in too good a mood to be bothered by the dwarf's quip. She could be heard to say "I'll treat you later" to Lizard Priest, so maybe she really had won her bet.

"Sweet nectar!" Lizard Priest exclaimed, slapping his tail against the grandstand, drawing surprised looks from the other spectators.

"..."

Priestess glanced at Baturu, who wasn't saying anything. Her still-young face was painted with displeasure. She'd remained sullen and silent ever since they had set out for the arena. Priestess was trying to decide whether to say something to her, but before she could come to a conclusion, Goblin Slayer said, "So what does this have to do with the so-called Silver Blaze?" His voice was cold, almost mechanical.

He must have found the competition interesting, for he had watched it without a word.

Right. Female Merchant nodded politely, then glanced around them.

"It's fine," Goblin Slayer said. "With this much chatter, it would be all the harder for anyone to hear what we were saying."

"Very well… You said this centaur you're looking for is a beautiful woman with a silver star streaking across her bangs."

"That's what I've heard," Goblin Slayer replied, nodding. Priestess noticed him glance at Baturu from under his helmet. The centaur girl's ears twitched, but of course she didn't say anything.

"Silver Blaze is one of the competitors here, someone with exactly the features you describe."

"Hoh."

"A young up-and-comer with fantastic legs. Everyone was excited to find out what kind of competitor she would be…," Female Merchant said before whispering grimly, "but then she disappeared to who knows where."

Some claimed—this was just a claim—that it had been the night of the storm some days ago. They said a suspicious man had come to the dormitory where the centaurs were who hadn't participated in the race, looking insistently for "quality." The lanistas, seeing that the man looked like a no-good gambler, set the dogs on him and drove him away.

But when everyone woke up the next morning…

"…They realized Silver Blaze wasn't in the dorm. Her personal lanista was missing, too."

"Surely they could simply have searched for them? Would they not have found them quickly?"

"They did conduct a search, but…they failed to locate her, unfortunately."

The other lanistas had immediately started looking for Silver Blaze in a furor. She was far and away the most beautiful of the centaurs—very distinctive. They should have found her easily.

"But all they found was the corpse of her trainer, lying on the edge of town, his skull split open."

Now, that sounds like the start of an adventure, Priestess thought, and she wasn't really wrong.

Goblin Slayer grunted softly, and the other members of the party exchanged thoughtful looks.

"Okay," said High Elf Archer, blinking. "So is that gambler the culprit or something?"

"I'm afraid we don't know," Female Merchant replied. Her words were direct, but her expression was one of ambivalence and concern. She cast glances right and left. "The gambler was apprehended promptly, but he swore up and down he didn't do it…"

"Feh! So does every two-bit lowlife!" Dwarf Shaman said, taking a gulp of his wine. In the arena, they were already preparing for the next competition; the sand had been cleaned up and the dirt packed back down. "But you've got your Lady Archbishop round here, haven't you?"

"Yes, but it's not as if she's personally involved in every investigation."

Which was not to say specifically that she wasn't involved in this one. This was the water town, after all, on the very knees of the Temple of Law that shouldered the responsibility for Order on the frontier. With Sword Maiden standing before them—she of the All Stars, the six heroes so beloved of the Supreme God—there was no one who would be able to pull off a lie.

"We asked a cleric of the Supreme God to invoke the Sense Lie miracle," Female Merchant said.

"And…?" How had it turned out? Priestess was eager to know.

"It was no good. I don't mean the miracle; I'm sure that was quite valid. The man insisted he knew nothing of the incident and had nothing to do with it, and that seems to be the truth."

"So you still don't have any idea who did it…?"

"No, and there were few footprints, which has meant plenty of rumors going around."

Maybe it was the doing of the birdfolk! No, a demon appeared and took her away! Or maybe some other agent of evil? Maybe it was some kind of snatcher, a doppelgänger or a snark. The story had long been told of the hunter who, in one night, killed six monsters who had disguised themselves as people in order to infiltrate human society. There were some things in this Four-Cornered World that simply brooked no credence.

"Does anyone really think it's the doing of the diamond knight?" Female Merchant asked, scowling. "People believe the stupidest things."

"Perhaps a dragon has taken her away to his cave," Lizard Priest quipped, earning him a "come on!" and a jab of the elbow from High Elf Archer (a jab he hardly noticed). In any case, it was true that there were many sources and forces of Chaos slithering around the Four-Cornered World, fishy and suspicious actors beyond number.

"There was even talk of bringing in a consulting detective from the capital," Female Merchant said.

"Consulting detective..." It was either High Elf Archer or Priestess who mumbled the words, finding them unfamiliar.

Female Merchant giggled and smiled. "There's been one soliciting work recently."

Oh...

Female Merchant was able to smile despite the painful brand still present on the nape of her neck, which she sometimes reached up through her hair to scratch. To see her show such pleasure, like any other girl her age, brought almost a sense of salvation to Priestess.

She realized how precious it all was.

It was this realization that prevented her from leaving Baturu to her own devices. "My princess would never do something so degrading," the centaur grumbled. No doubt she was looking up now, glaring, unable to take any more. She was staring straight at the centaurs who had entered the arena moments before. They were waving to the cheering crowd, strutting around, prideful and beautiful. Or at least, so they looked to Priestess...

"Those girls are being put on display! Have they no shame?" Baturu demanded.

"I don't think they're doing anything dishonorable," Priestess ventured, but Baturu appeared to disagree. No matter how they tried to see eye to eye, humans and centaurs were just different, and sometimes different things simply didn't match up. They could walk side by side, but they would never be quite in step.

"I've heard the Valkyrie herself was once a sword fighter," Priestess offered.

"I neither know nor care about your human gods," Baturu snapped, and there wasn't much Priestess could say to that. Instead, the centaur continued: "I have no idea who this Silver Blaze actually is, but my princess would never stoop so low as to—"

"If you're so sure about that, would you like to meet one of them?"

It was Priestess's friend Female Merchant who threw this lifeline. She looked Baturu in the eyes, just as Priestess had—indeed, Female Merchant had learned by watching her friend. Even with her large, equine body, when she was seated, the centaur warrior was not so much taller than a delicate human female (Baturu herself seemed a bit on the small side among centaurs).

Female Merchant saw confusion mingled with anger in Baturu's eyes. She offered a small smile. "I don't mean Silver Blaze, of course. But one of our aurigae was close to her."

"If nothing else, we must confirm whether this Silver Blaze was the centaur princess," Goblin Slayer said—businesslike, and no more, as ever. At the same time, however, he seemed to be saying that a shouting match here would solve nothing.

Baturu cast a barbed glare in the direction of the metal helmet. Priestess, as well as the other party members, knew quite well that Goblin Slayer meant only and exactly what he said. They looked at each other and grinned. They could try to explain, but it seemed likely to just antagonize Baturu more. Better to keep things moving along. That was one excellent reason to leave this matter to the party leader…

Except he doesn't actually realize, does he?

He was truly hopeless. He preached the importance of swift decision-making but didn't believe that he did it himself.

Goblin Slayer was silent for a moment, seemingly considering the way his companions were looking at him. When he spoke, though, it was in the same unflappable tone, with the same decisiveness: "Show us there, if you would."

§

The maidens who gathered in the garden of the Valkyrie and the Trade God, the gods of the true path, rushed along the racecourse, illuminating the garden with their smiles. They wore dark-colored training uniforms, their hearts as pure and true as their bodies. They ran, beautifully, the hair of their tails never disheveled, their pointed ears never laid back. What could be more natural?

Needless to say, none of these young ladies was so uncouth as to let her horseshoes clatter as she ran.

The competitors' *ludus*—their training grounds—was located within the precincts of the water town, not far from the arena.

Priestess breathed a sigh of relief as she extricated herself from the still-buzzing crowd of spectators. Gondolas plied the river as they walked alongside it, and she was surprised to discover that this alone was enough to calm her down.

The place Female Merchant brought them was indeed appropriate to be called a *ludus*, which also meant school. A red-roofed building was surrounded on four sides by what looked like the walls of a fortification, surrounding an inner courtyard. Training tools of all kinds waited within, and there was even a practice racecourse.

"All right, listen up! You have to create an hourglass within yourself! *You* have to understand your own pace, how fast you're going!"

"Yes, sir!"

"Why're you trying to get out in front? Hang back and conserve your energy! Everyone fall in; we're going to keep practicing our side-by-side running!"

"Yes, sir!"

"All right, first, take a break," said another voice. "Make sure you get plenty of water. Anyone feeling ill?"

"I'm all right!" one person responded.

"I think one of my horseshoes is coming off..."

"Make sure you get it secured posthaste. That goes for all of you—if you want to win, take the best possible care of your legs!"

"Hey, your tail is looking a little scruffy."

"Oh! I'm s-sorry..."

"Listen, even the gods are watching us. We've got to be presentable."

The lanistas, who were distinguished by the wooden swords they carried, could be heard instructing the racers. The centaurs responded with vigor, perspiration was shed, and everyone pushed and fought for anything that might make them even a fraction faster.

What most surprised Priestess was the presence of other centaurs, not just humans, among the lanistas. Although it made sense: Humans had only two legs; they wouldn't know how to run with four like a centaur.

"Ah, the passion! Most admirable," Lizard Priest said, smiling at the scene. "I am put in mind of the training barracks in my own village."

He continued mumbling to himself ("Soldiers who would stand side by side must be from the same barracks or at least from a place of similar capacities") as Female Merchant bowed shyly to him. "I appreciate your saying so. Things are finally going more or less according to plan..."

To have an accomplished warrior like this lizardman praise the establishment was more than an honor for a human. Who could blame Female Merchant if she allowed herself a little smile? Indeed, it was only natural.

"So, *'hem*," Dwarf Shaman said, looking up at her, "this is your place, then?"

"I acquired it shortly after it began operating. An acquaintance sold it to me at a bargain price—they felt it was better than seeing the place go to waste." Looking back on it now, she could see there might have been an element of friendly affection at work—but only looking back on it. For when a scarred young woman suddenly reappeared and went into business, the pushback was severe.

It often wasn't enough simply to make a profit and earn back an investment. Female Merchant was coming to understand that much of the loathing for nobles' games stemmed not from lofty ideals but from sheer lack of understanding. So it was that the same crowd who cheered and celebrated at the coliseum would kick the proverbial sand at the people involved as they walked away. She understood she mustn't get too attached, become too obsessed, but still...

"I know but little about all this, but I've managed to come this far, thankfully," she said.

Still, she felt she was justified in a measure of pride, that this couldn't be called a mere diversion for her.

"Sure, it's terrific. Lots of things never do go according to plan, after all!" Dwarf Shaman laughed, showing his teeth. Female Merchant still felt rather flattered.

Her touch of embarrassment was perfectly natural, but far be it from the sharp eyes of High Elf Archer to miss it. "What? What? Are you planning to make adventurers compete, too?"

"Ah, that might be a good idea," Female Merchant said merrily. "That dungeoneering contest turned out to be such a success, after all…"

"Oh, please, don't. Something you just show up and whip through is no adventure. She'd just be mass-producing Orcbolgs," the elf quipped. This provoked a guffaw from Female Merchant (a polite, girlish guffaw).

The subject of the chuckling himself showed no sign of being either bothered or interested.

I'm not sure what to think… Priestess found herself smiling, too, but also a little embarrassed; she shifted uncomfortably. Her anxiety about her own inexperience hadn't disappeared yet, but she couldn't help wondering if they saw her that way, too. Although she was very happy to see one of her dear friends succeed so well.

Without warning, Goblin Slayer spoke up. "Now," he said, his tone diffident as ever. "About Silver Blaze."

"Oh yes, of course," said Female Merchant. "Pardon me." She coughed, her cheeks reddening, and she glanced around the training area. Her eyes soon lit on one person in particular, and she called her name, a name of Lightning.

Yes, Lightning: It was the centaur who had appeared with the suddenness of a thunderclap at the end of the race earlier. She was lovely and distinguished, with black hair and her mane tied neatly behind her head in a single braid. Her figure was clearly visible as she approached; Priestess had had an inkling from the spectator seating, but now she was sure:

She's…big.

The thought came unbidden to her mind as she looked at the centaur woman. As at the race, her outfit revealed a toned, trained body. She wore a look of determination, and with the red sash she was wearing, she had the bearing of a prince. Still, the curves visible under her training outfit were unmistakably womanly; she had an allure much like Sword Maiden's.

The centaur approached with a gentle clop of horseshoes, and Female Merchant engaged her in friendly conversation. "You're running already? The race just finished."

"I'm merely cooling down. I'm not pushing myself; don't worry."

"How are your legs?"

"Nothing to be concerned about."

If Priestess felt a touch of surprise, it was because something seemed off about the centaur's gait. Running at full speed must put a substantial burden on their legs.

When the racer noticed Priestess glancing at her limbs, she came over and took her hand easily, bringing it gently to her lips. "Might I ask what I can help you with, my young lady?"

"Eep!" Priestess squeaked when the dashing centaur greeted her as respectfully as if she were nobility.

I mean... Of course I'm surprised, right...?

"We want to know about Silver Blaze." The voice was calmness itself, and it brought strenuous relief to Priestess as it spoke on her behalf. For the racer's eyes had glittered like lightning, so irresistibly beautiful that Priestess had almost been sucked into them. She could have gazed at them for eternity, at risk of her life. Instead she was instantly smitten, and that alone seemed to be enough.

"Silver Blaze?" The golden eyes blinked. "Are you fans of hers? I daresay one could get jealous!" Her gaze took in the dwarf, the lizardman, the figure in the grimy armor—and then she stopped beside him. "So even a high elf is in the thrall of our Blaze? I'm sure if you saw *me* run, I might sway your affections..."

"We saw you," High Elf Archer said, laughter chuckling in her throat. "And you were beautiful, truly."

"You are too kind. If you wish, I could be moved to give a private demonstration run for you..."

Female Merchant mouthed, *All right, enough*, though she didn't say anything. (*Some people*, she appeared to add, *have no constancy*.)

At that, the racer's lightning eyes sparkled with mischief, and her lips moved alluringly. "Oh, don't get all upset. My worthy opponents won't let me live it down if they get all the attention at the track."

"I can't believe this. And you've got a race to run!"

"Aw, going to kick me out for being insolent?"

"I can't—can't believe this..." Female Merchant had her head in her hands, while the racer laughed uproariously. It was almost hard to tell whether they were joking around or not. The racer looked free and easy, but it was clear there was more to her than that. No one who was simply frivolous could ever learn to run like she could.

Another voice spoke up: "There's no way it was the princess..." It was Baturu, staring at the ground. She was murmuring, but the racer certainly heard her. "The princess would never wish to put herself on *display* on some other thing than grass..."

"Grass? You mean turf? Only the Circus in the capital has that—too much trouble to be forever replanting it and keeping it up around here." The racer trotted over to Baturu's side, kneeling slightly to look her in the face. "If you're running on turf, you're running in the capital. I'd love to try it myself someday... But perhaps you feel I shouldn't?"

"...!"

Baturu gave a sharp intake of breath, her cheeks flushing with heightened emotion. Tears beaded at the corners of her eyes. She tossed her head up and exclaimed, "A-aren't you ashamed?! To be...? To do...?"

"I have my modesty, of course. I grant I was more than a little nervous the first time I ran in front of an audience."

"That's not what I meant!"

"Ha-ha-ha." All Baturu's yelling seemed to roll right off her back. The eyes that crackled with lightning fixed the young girl in place. "I come from a long line of runners. Like my parents... Well, my mother was anonymous." But her father, she said, was a famous racer who had won many prizes. Her eyes squinted in a smile; she sounded downright proud of it. "So I tell you, in all my races, I have never felt shame about the blood that flows in my veins. Never once."

To that, not even Baturu had an answer. Instead, she opened her mouth, then closed it, and finally she bit her lip, looking at the ground. "But the princess...," she said.

When the racer reached out to run a hand gently through her hair, Baturu didn't push her away. Even as she patted Baturu's head, the racer's lightning eyes flickered in the direction of the other adventurers. "This princess—was it Silver Blaze?"

"We don't know," said Goblin Slayer. "That's what we were hoping to find out."

"Hmm… Perhaps you could describe her for me?"

"We only know what we've heard," Priestess said, but she offered what she could on behalf of Baturu, who couldn't look up, couldn't even speak. No one in the party remarked on the droplets spilling from her eyes onto the ground in front of her. Neither, of course, did the centaur with the lightning eyes.

"That description—yes, it does sound like her," the centaur said when she was told of the lock of silver hair that shot like a comet across the princess's brow. "She was a lovely young lady. She ran so comfortably. And she was a princess? I suppose it would explain much…"

"How do you mean?" Priestess asked.

"She had…a nobility about her. The way she carried herself was impeccable. Does that make sense?"

"I see…" Priestess looked at High Elf Archer, then at Female Merchant, and she thought of King's Sister, who wasn't there at that moment. Compared with her, the way they held themselves was—well, it was completely different. "Yes. That makes perfect sense."

"She say anything 'bout how she came to be in these parts?" Dwarf Shaman asked.

The lightning-eyed racer's ears took on an uneasy cant. "Well, she was with a different *ludus*. And we've only met on the track a few times…" The centaur put a hand to her chin thoughtfully; she almost looked like an actor playing a part. Her other hand never stopped gently stroking Baturu's head, though it was obvious she was thinking hard. "I must say, though, she never seemed to want to talk much about her past. We always spoke of racing."

"But surely you must have heard something?" Female Merchant asked, touching the racer's flank in a gesture of intimacy. "I know you always want to chat when you see a new girl. Even if you're not serious about it."

The answer didn't come immediately. The shouting of the other centaurs rushing around the inner courtyard echoed this way and that, mingling with the voices of the lanistas. A particularly emphatic gust of wind stirred up the courtyard's dust and stagnant air.

After a long moment, something seemed to shift in those lightning eyes. They closed slowly, and the centaur exhaled. "Just to be clear, what I'm about to say is no comment on her racing. I want you to understand that."

"I've never seen Silver Blaze race," Goblin Slayer said brusquely. "And what I haven't seen, I cannot comment on."

That seemed to satisfy the centaur. Something like a smile entered her eyes. "I was told she came from a coachman."

"Coachman?"

"Someone who sells centaurs for a living. They lead their victims on with promises that they'll take them somewhere fun and exciting." And once the centaurs are convinced that they're going to a joyous Pleasure Island, they're sold as simple, stupid donkeys.

The price of ignorance for a naive youngster who just wants to get away from the herd and live in freedom is always great. Although any adventurer would understand that there are certain things you can't obtain if you don't take the risk.

"The selling of slaves as such isn't illegal," Female Merchant noted, adding quietly that some people at some *ludi* must buy them without knowing where they came from.

A person might find themselves enslaved for many reasons: They might be captured in war or fail to pay a debt, or it might be punishment for a crime. All one had to do was work industriously until one had bought one's freedom—no particular problem with that. In every time and every place, however, there were those who would abuse the system.

"This is sounding more and more like an urban adventure," High Elf Archer said with a "hmm," although she added in a whisper that she wasn't thrilled about that. She acted as if she was thinking about something profound and important, but the human world was always a complicated and confusing place to the high elves. She quickly abandoned any real attempt to deduce anything, instead smacking her party leader gently on the back. "I think this is your department, Orcbolg. The whole thing beats the heck out of me."

"I'm not very knowledgeable in such things myself."

Yeah, right! High Elf Archer snorted again, but she, too, felt like she was grasping at thin air; it was all a mystery. The party members looked at one another, but no answer was forthcoming.

"So what's your feeling—does this have anything to do with that murdered lanista and the kidnapping?" Dwarf Shaman asked.

"I suppose it seems likely that he was killed because he was seen trying to abduct her," Priestess offered.

"I must point out that at the moment, we have no positive evidence that this Silver Blaze is indeed the princess we seek," Lizard Priest said.

"We don't know for sure." The helmet shook side to side. "But we have information. We can do what we can."

That would seem to imply that this slayer of goblins had a next step in mind.

Good by me, then.

High Elf Archer, satisfied with this conclusion for her own part, glanced over at Baturu to see if her heightened emotions were finally starting to come down. The small centaur was rubbing her eyes; she slowly looked up to meet the lightning eyes of the other woman.

"Then…you're saying that the princess was among those who were tricked and…and sold?"

"I'm afraid I can't speak to that with any certainty. All I know is…" The tall centaur almost trailed off—not because anything dark loomed over them but out of compassion. One more time, she ran her fingers through the smaller girl's hair. "All I know is the grace with which she ran." She then added, "Though you may not wish to hear it."

"No," Baturu said, shaking her head, her mane fluttering with it. "I see now that you run with your whole heart. I saw it myself, and still I belittled you. For that, I can only apologize."

"It's all right. If a cute girl's talking to me, I'm happy no matter what she says." The centaur with the lightning eyes smiled broadly. The expression fit her gallant features perfectly, yet it also had a girlish innocence. It was like a blossoming flower, and rather than exuding maturity, it made you realize how young she was. "If you want to clear your conscience, come cheer for me! I would love to dedicate a victory to a lovely young thing like you."

"I…I wish you wouldn't tease me…," Baturu said. Girlish the centaur might be, but her behavior could be hard to watch.

At Baturu's stammering response (accompanied by a blush in the cheeks), the other woman's grin turned to something more mischievous. Even a few of the centaur girls practicing their running had stopped to stare—it was too much.

"Goodness gracious!" Lizard Priest said, shaking his long head in admiration, his eyes rolling. "You are a fair lady indeed! If you were a lizardman, I doubt I could keep my claws off you!"

High Elf Archer puffed out her cheeks—what was he even saying?—and jabbed him in the side.

"Most unfortunately," replied the centaur, one of those lightning-shimmering eyes closing in a wink, "I'm partial to comely lasses myself."

Oh, for…

This time it was Female Merchant's turn to pout in exasperation.

§

"I'm going out for a bit," Goblin Slayer said. "What will you do?"

"I'll go with you!" Priestess said promptly.

They had just gotten back from the aurigae *ludus*. The sun was getting lower in the sky, twilight spreading out above their heads. Night surged in like a wave, soon to swallow the town.

High Elf Archer was watching it from the window, looking thoughtful—a vision that could have been a painting in its own right. "I'll stay here. I'm pretty tired," she said, her jade eyes flitting over to the corner where Baturu knelt. "And I'd like to have a little chat."

"Are you sure about that…?" Priestess asked.

"What's to be sure about? It is what it is. Don't give it another thought." High Elf Archer waved at Priestess, who nodded. Instead of leaving Baturu stuck with her all the time, maybe it would help to have someone else try to talk to her once in a while.

In fact, I'm convinced.

There might be ways that an elf was closer to Baturu than a human like her was.

The conversation inspired Dwarf Shaman and Lizard Priest to share a quick glance and a nod. "S'pose we'd better try chatting with those lanistas, eh, Scaly?" Dwarf Shaman said.

"Mm, indeed. I think if we can find somewhere to treat them to a drink, they should be quite forthcoming," Lizard Priest agreed. High Elf Archer giggled—it sounded like he just wanted a bite to eat—but her laughter was nothing malicious. It was just the usual humor between party members.

Goblin Slayer gazed around at the group, then said soberly, "Very well. I'll trust you to take care of things."

Though there was much Priestess still didn't know, she had the impression that this was how urban adventures went—in other words, just as on a regular adventure, they each had their own role to play.

Come to think of it…

She realized it had been the same on their last adventure in the water town (that had been quite a while ago), and the thought brought a smile to her face.

The town streaked with twilight. The gondolas floating lazily along the canals. The sweet, cold ice treat. Somehow she only ever seemed to come here on adventures, and she'd never had a chance to just take in the sights.

"Still, I think the place seems calmer than before," she said.

"Is that so?"

"Uh-huh." She nodded as they walked along the road. "It's just… sort of a feeling."

"I see."

It was probably because they had been able to drive out the goblins. That was certainly, unquestionably a good thing.

There was an ever so slight touch of softness in Goblin Slayer's voice as he walked beside her, and it made Priestess's steps lighter.

Even so, walking a new road in a city she didn't know very well could be more confusing than delving a dungeon. Everywhere she looked, there were flagstones and stone buildings, and the burbling of water came from everywhere at once. She had been so engaged in walking along with Goblin Slayer that she no longer knew where she was. If she'd been told at that moment to go back to the Temple, she didn't think she could have made it. The racetrack was somewhere in town, too, yet she wasn't sure where that might be, either. Instead, she worked hard to keep pace with Goblin Slayer as he strode through the roads.

The shadows of the looming buildings grew ever longer, quavering as the last light of day faded away.

"So, um, where are we going?" Priestess asked.

"I don't know."

"You...you don't?"

That seemed to be the entirety of his explanation. Priestess couldn't hold back a frown, and if Guild Girl had been there, she probably would have smiled wryly. Maybe only Cow Girl, waiting for his return back on the frontier, could have taken this answer with a straight face.

"Ah. No, that's not what I mean," Goblin Slayer added, evidently recognizing Priestess's concern. "I have landmarks."

"Landmarks?"

Goblin Slayer pointed to a chalk streak etched on the road, a tiny symbol. It would look like a child's scribble if you hadn't been told about it or didn't know what you were looking for.

Oh! Out of the flotsam of Priestess's memories, an insight presented itself. "Is that from the Rogues Guild?"

"It's a sign," Goblin Slayer said. "Passed down, or so it's said, from the Gray Wizard himself."

The Rouges Guild—an association of criminals. A gathering of the unsavory and the underhanded. Priestess felt herself go stiff. It wasn't that she specifically disliked the Rogues Guild—they'd helped her more than once.

But it's...only natural to be a little nervous, right...?

"You're sure they won't mind you following their trail?" she asked.

"They would tell me if there was a problem."

His words were brief, piercing—yet Priestess happily said, "Right!"

and nodded enthusiastically. For it meant she only had to follow and trust him.

With her experience, of course, she didn't have to study the symbol in detail, let alone sketch it for herself. No sooner had she seen it than she was carving it into her memory.

What must Goblin Slayer have thought as Priestess followed him like an enthusiastic puppy? He was not one to be uncomfortable with silence—so his thoughtful quiet at that moment meant he was searching for the words.

Finally he said, "There is no particular need for you to remember that symbol. This method isn't necessary for all adventurers."

"It isn't?"

"I needed it. So I learned about it." Goblin Slayer took another corner at his nonchalant stride, heading for an intersection. He didn't look back, but Priestess followed him dutifully. "As for you, you need only find a scout to be in your party."

His advice was very brief—did that mean someone other than himself? Priestess didn't quite understand. Did it mean he envisioned her leaving this party someday?

But that…

It seemed both eminently reasonable and completely unimaginable at the same time. Or wait, maybe he was simply referring to the times she'd temporarily teamed up with another party.

Hrm…

Yes, that has to be it, Priestess told herself. This person always said what he meant. There were no hidden meanings lurking behind his words. Priestess thought she understood that much.

"However, you should be aware that such things exist," he said.

Priestess responded earnestly: "Right."

They seemed to be heading ever farther into a dark alleyway, yet the farther along they went, the livelier it seemed to get.

I wonder if we're getting near the main street.

And so it turned out the place Goblin Slayer had brought her to was no seamy back alley. Instead it was a part of the town that was sophisticated, pretty, and calming, not unlike the arena they'd visited earlier that day. There were classy inns and restaurants from which the alluring aromas of fancy cuisine emanated.

Beyond those places, there was another—a building so large and so elegant, it could have been mistaken for a king's mansion: the casino.

§

When they entered the casino, for a moment, Priestess simply stopped and stared. It was all completely new to her. She had never heard so many coins jangling at once. She quickly realized that the source of the sound wasn't actual money but small chips that were doing their best impression of currency. Even so, they must have represented a far greater sum than she had ever seen in one place in her life.

Populating the building were gentlemen and ladies of every sort, from every people group, wearing a dizzying array of fancy outfits. Goblin Slayer was leading her farther within, but Priestess's eyes were going in every direction at every turn. Here there was a table covered in green felt, with chips sliding back and forth across it; there, dice were being rolled. Over in another corner, there was a racetrack small enough to fit on a table; a closer look revealed that players were racing with centaur-shaped pawns. They would lay down chips to advance their pieces, and occasionally cries of *"Ave Caesar!"* would ring out.

Maybe it was always more exciting to do something than to watch it. Humans couldn't run like centaurs, after all.

Some people were tossing five dice hoping for matching faces; others rolled three skulls. Another game that appeared to be growing heated was one in which two pawns shaped like sword fighters closed in on each other. Just when you thought all the pawns must be riflemen with repeaters held aloft, you would notice pawns like beautiful goddesses, too. One thing all these games had in common: They were every one of them long-lived board games with a tradition and a history.

Many of them, though, were quite strange. Priestess was particularly intrigued by one that was about trying to get as much loot as you could out of a trap-filled dungeon. The deeper you went, the more treasure you could get, but the more traps there would be—and the bigger the chance to lose it all.

Another thing that set Priestess's eyes spinning was the profusion of beautiful and highly exposed young women. For a second, she thought they were harefolk, but then she would see human ears, or elf or dwarf ears, peeking out from their heads. So the rabbit ears were just some sort of accessory…

We certainly couldn't bring her *here*, Priestess reflected, thinking of the friend who waited back at the Temple as she took in the panoply of games. But then again, some of her other friends, like High Elf Archer or Female Merchant, would definitely enjoy themselves in this place. Even if Priestess could practically see Baturu frowning…

"…Do you suppose they have hnefatafl here?" she said, the thought occurring to her suddenly. It was the game she had played—and very much enjoyed—up north.

"You're curious about these games? Would you like to play?"

"Oh, no, I couldn't…" She waved her hands vigorously. She hadn't expected such a response from Goblin Slayer. He seemed like he might practically be about to give her some money to take to the tables, and what would that make her but a child getting her allowance?

Besides…

They were an adventurer in grimy armor, striding along, and a priestess in a dusty cloak, keeping pace through a sophisticated place of entertainment. Looks of disdain came their way from every direction, which Priestess noted with a sense of intimidation. She could tell she didn't belong here, and she gripped her sounding staff firmly in both hands.

"*Ahem*, but anyway… Couldn't we have come here from the main street?"

"The question is not where you're going but how you get there," Goblin Slayer said. It was like a riddle.

No, Priestess thought, it wasn't *like* a riddle; it *was* a riddle. They had taken a roundabout route, following a series of mysterious symbols to get here—that had to be some sort of signal. For behold…

"Greetings, esteemed patron," said a handsome man in a black suit, presumably an employee of the casino, who approached without a sound. Priestess had enough experience from her various adventures to guess that this man must have trained as a scout. He greeted them as courteously as if they were members of the royal family. "This way, my good sir. And your friend...?"

"Hrm," Goblin Slayer said, but he didn't answer immediately. Priestess continued clutching her staff and tried standing up straighter. Finally he said, "Today, I want you to get used to this place."

"Oh, y-yes, sir!" Priestess said, thrilled that he hadn't said *wait here* or *stay behind*. Instead she felt it was an affirmation that she could learn much by watching things here. She bowed deeply in polite farewell, and Goblin Slayer walked off. The employee went alongside him, showing him into a back area of the casino.

From under his helmet, Goblin Slayer's eyes flitted toward the man in the suit. "Would you be so kind as to keep an eye on her?"

"But of course, my dear patron. I had every intention."

"Of course you did."

It should have gone without saying. But these days, he felt he found himself saying more and more things that could have gone without being said. After all, the girl had scolded him so many times to the effect that if he didn't say something, his message would never get across.

Which implies...

That he was maturing, yes? Growing? He wasn't sure—but perhaps. If nothing else, the girl was certainly learning and growing. Enough so that he had hesitated to take her into the back here. The place behind the flashy, splashy gambling venue. The innermost room at the end of the twisting maze of hallways.

It was worth knowing that places like this existed, and how to use them if you needed them—but not more than that.

The place was like a private room at the back of a restaurant, quiet and calm—but there wasn't a single window. There were tables that looked as if they were just waiting for food and drinks that might come out at any moment—but there were no glasses on them.

Goblin Slayer sat on one side of the table, the man in a suit on the other. The man extended his hand politely, and Goblin Slayer responded mechanically.

"Now, good sir, why not take it easy? Enjoy yourself."

"Thank you, I will. Since you've offered me a chair and a cup, I shall introduce myself. Please relax."

"I appreciate your introducing yourself. As you can see, I am a man of but little etiquette, and I must beg your indulgence."

"And I am dressed for business, as you can see, so I must beg *your* indulgence."

"No, no, I must insist you relax."

"No, *you* relax."

"Well, if you insist, then I will, gratefully. I hope you don't mind my relaxing first."

"You must excuse my uncivilized appearance. I come from a pioneer town on the western frontier; my master was he who rides on barrels and my profession is the slaying of goblins."

"I believe this is the first time we've met. With apologies, I will speak on behalf of the madam. I am the owner of The Mermaid."

"Thank you for accepting my introduction. Please raise your head."

"Of course, dear sir, but raise *your* head first."

"That would be problematic."

"At the same time, then."

"That is acceptable."

"The request is humbly made, then."

It was a careful, ritualized exchange. Quick, but always polite, greetings exchanged with every concern for courtesy. After a moment, they both lifted their hands and looked each other in the face.

"I'm surprised you felt this required the owner's personal attention," Goblin Slayer said.

"One would never wish to risk appearing rude to a Silver-ranked adventurer," the man replied, scrutinizing Goblin Slayer's helmet just enough that it wouldn't be impolite. "Let alone the pupil of Burglar, He Who Rides Barrels."

"My teacher...," Goblin Slayer began and then corrected himself. "My master is my master. I don't seek to borrow his influence."

"Does one not use everything that one can?"

"I appreciate that, but if I wore his name down to where it could no longer be used, I would be yelled at for it."

"Very well, then." The man's courteous smile never faltered. "You are the one who has the affections of our Lady Sword Maiden, the one who killed the goblins in the city sewers, my dear patron."

Goblin Slayer groaned quietly, less than amused to be addressed this way. No matter how he sliced it, it was too grand a name for him. He was no famous master of the sword.

"Can our runners be of use to you?" the man asked.

"No, I'm here for information," Goblin Slayer replied.

"We do sell that, of course."

"I'm looking for a lost centaur. It involves a..." Goblin Slayer gazed into empty space as if hoping to find the word there. At least it was easier to remember than the name of a monster. "...a coachman."

"Ah. Silver Blaze." The employee of the casino—no, of the Rogues Guild—nodded knowingly. "Yes, we were worried about her, too. The gamblers did have such a soft spot for her."

He clapped his hands, summoning someone. A moment later, a young woman in an outfit that didn't look rogue-like at all appeared in the doorway bearing food. Signature dishes from the water town: fish and shrimp that had been steamed or fried or something in oil. There was grape wine, too. The fact that both cups were poured from the same jug was no doubt a gesture of goodwill on the part of the Rogues Guild. Goblin Slayer, however, quietly declined the drink.

"I'm in the middle of a job," he explained. Besides: "I have heard that after this is over, my party will eat together."

"Pardon us. Yes, of course. If you'll excuse me, then..." The employee took a small sip of his own wine, just enough to wet his lips. "As it happens, racing centaurs disappear with a certain regularity. It's not as uncommon as you might think."

This was his explanation:

Sometimes a racer who was rewriting the record books would be abducted and disappeared as a way of striking against their master's business. Or a centaur might be in transit when their lanista was killed, and they found themselves sold to someone in the area. Or a *ludus* might go bankrupt and its centaurs run away in the night, or they might be put up as security on the mortgage and all of them be taken away somewhere at a stroke.

There was nothing unusual about centaurs being caught up in human disputes in this way. And of course there were slave traders who might become illegally involved in the middle of it all. Yes, they existed, but…

"But all that's hardly something that happens only to centaurs. Even if their plight does seem to attract a particular type of bleeding heart."

"I understand."

What were they supposed to do—stop the centaurs from running? It wasn't possible. These were people who were born to run. If you had seen them, vivacious and beautiful as they raced around the arena, you knew that. Though many of them might never reach the very top, the coliseum was still a place of honor and of dreams.

To tell the centaurs never to run again—wouldn't that be even crueler than kidnapping them? It would be like telling an adventurer not to go on adventures because they were dangerous. Yes, there were probably those among the racers who had been sold into it as slaves. But then, there were adventurers who had taken up the trade for lack of any other choice. No one had the right to cast aspersions on someone else's path in life. Even Goblin Slayer could understand that much.

"However, I'm not here to ask about the coachman or who kidnapped Silver Blaze," he said.

"Hoh," responded the man in the suit.

"If it was a question that could be answered by asking, Silver Blaze would already be in the arena racing."

"I agree entirely."

"That's why I'm here on this…" There, Goblin Slayer stopped. He still hesitated to speak the word *adventure*. Instead he said, "What I want to know about…is goblins."

INTERLUDE

Be Careful of Your Contacts

"Senior! Senior! You *have* to trade with me!"

"Who, me…?"

The red-haired elf sounded particularly flummoxed as the other girls came rushing into the cabaret. The elf wore a very revealing leather outfit, rabbit ears that bobbed over her head, and even a puffy white tail on her behind. She'd just been checking herself out in the mirror—most inconvenient timing.

Even I have to admit…

Her body really wasn't much to look at. But she was on a run, so there was no choice. If there was one silver lining, it was that it seemed to please the boy who'd been running with her for so long.

In any case, the reason for the blush on the face of the adventurer who served the Supreme God wasn't the costumes.

"I'm not sure I can stand to be seen this way…!"

"Can't say I think lookin' like this is any cause for concern," said another girl who had been all but dragged into the room. White ears floated above her head, too, but she wasn't wearing any gloves—the fur on her bare legs and arms proved that she was a real harefolk.

She'd hopped through the casino with such enthusiasm, the elf had worried she might bump into a customer.

She sure proved she could dodge people with the best of them, though.

The red-haired elf couldn't help being impressed—although she

©Noboru Kannatuki

didn't think she'd been in business so long as to warrant being called "Senior." She covered for herself with a discreet cough.

Trying her best to sound like the kind of trustworthy, more experienced operator the others could count on, she said, "What's the matter? Didn't that last customer tell you to follow him?"

"Yeah, he did, but..."

"He was just a young guy. Did you fight?"

"He was just relaxing out back. Forget him! Hmph!" The cleric of the Supreme God folded her arms, her voice turning sharp in an attempt to hide her embarrassment.

Pretty sure it was a three-person party, the elf thought, flipping the pages of her mental notebook. A warrior, a cleric, and a harefolk girl who was presumably a scout or a ranger. Security at the casino. A party of adventurers from the frontier, hired on a temporary basis.

Get someone local, and there was a good chance they would be a customer themselves. Wouldn't want them giving any breaks to any of the other players. So it wasn't unusual to occasionally look for security staff from outside Adventurers Guilds.

Anyway, that's what I hear.

From that perspective, she was something of an irregular herself. The red-haired elf smiled. "What, then? Did he try to pull anything? You could have called one of the enforcers..."

"He was a friend of mine..."

"...Oh." That was the one answer that could bring her up short.

I mean, I guess I understand how she's feeling...

The elf was the same way; if *that man* had shown up here as a customer, not knowing she was around, she wasn't sure how she would have reacted to him. It didn't even have to be him. If any of her other friends—the cleric of the God of Knowledge or that white creature—had shown up, she would have been frozen in place. Thankfully (she thought), they were each handling their own thing right now, so there was no chance they would stumble on her.

"It's just a job. Not like you're doing anything wrong. And I guess I'd be happy to meet an older girl I knew here," the harefolk girl said.

"I guess... It's true that ensuring fairness in gambling is one of the duties of the Supreme God." But this, the cleric averred, was entirely different from the outfit worn during the offertory at the harvest festival.

"Huh, that right?" the harefolk girl said, her ears bobbing merrily. "Well anyway, I'm hungry!"

"You padfoots seem to have it rough that way."

The red-haired elf muttered a self-motivating "okay!" and then stood up from the mirror. "You can have the baked treats here in the greenroom. I'll go out there for you."

"Hooray! Thanks a bunch!"

"I'm sorry, Senior. Thank you very much…!"

It was all right. It was fine. The senior (it stung a little to be called that) waved the girl's apologies away and exited the dressing room. *Gotta get out there eventually anyway*, she thought, but she refrained from saying as much to the other girls.

In any event, bedecked in her harefolk outfit (why *did* they dress that way around here?), she prepared to take that first step out into the casino.

The instant she got on the floor, she could feel the collective gaze of everyone in the casino slam into her.

It only feels that way… It only feels that way, she told herself.

This was a place of amusements, after all—probably 80 percent of the eyes here were focused firmly on some game or other. The games were classy, social; no one had to bet their lives or their livelihoods. The well-appointed ladies and gentlemen were probably most interested in the person hanging off their arm anyway, and besides, the elf was just one among many "harefolk" girls.

I need to look like I belong here.

Scampering around looking anxious would only serve to draw attention to her. With a scrape of the unfamiliar high heels across the floor, the red-haired elf set out, her elegant chest leading the way.

Okay, now, where was the seat of the customer she'd been instructed to find? She thought she remembered the number; it was— Oh, there she was.

Huddled there was a girl in cleric's vestments who looked distinctly out of place—not afraid so much as deeply interested in her surroundings; she sat in a chair provided for people to take a break and was looking avidly at everything going on around her. There was a sounding staff laid across her knees, which were in a perfect row. A priestess of the Earth Mother. An adventurer, no doubt. Golden hair. Cute.

"Wait..."

"Oh!"

The elf had never imagined the adventurer in question might be someone she knew, but she saw the flash of recognition in the face of the other young woman as she sat blinking at her.

"Er, we met out east, didn't we?" the cleric said.

"Yeah, fancy seeing you here. An adventurer, right?" The red-haired elf somehow managed to keep her face from twitching and smiled instead. She wasn't sure if she was blushing from embarrassment—she hoped the makeup, which she wore only rarely but was wearing today, would help if she was.

I guess in one way, it makes things easier.

She knew she wouldn't have to worry about any unfamiliar rules of etiquette with this person. Breathing a private sigh of relief, she sat down next to the priestess. "Here for fun?" she asked.

"No, business. Oh, um, not me personally, I mean. A member of my party."

"Oh yeah?" the red-haired elf said diffidently. She might have sounded disinterested, but she thought she had a pretty good sense of what was going on. After all, when they ran into each other in the desert country, she'd been at *that shop*. Much like now.

Guess they've got dealings with the underworld.

Well, so did she. Maybe it was only natural—or unavoidable—that they would find each other again.

"What brings you here, if I may ask...?" the priestess said.

"I guess you could say business, too. This and that."

The red-haired elf smiled ambiguously. It wasn't a lie, not really. Anyway, she didn't think most clerics would be suspicious enough to go around brandishing Sense Lie at everyone, even as a bluff. How could a cleric who didn't even trust people ever trust the gods? That went double for her friend the cleric.

At the same time, runners needed to be able to tame their private obsessions.

And practically speaking, expenses are a real problem…

It inevitably cost a great deal of money for a sorcerer to arrange the cards in their hand, even if a black lotus wasn't the first thing they drew.

"…This place is really impressive," the priestess said, politely refraining from inquiring further into the elf's personal situation as she cast her eye around the casino. At some point, a huge glass tub full of water had been brought out from somewhere within the building. "I've never seen such a large box made of glass. Is that what they call…an aquarium?"

"Yeah. A mermaid dancer is gonna do a show. Tonight's performance should start in a few minutes."

"Wow…!"

That was why they called this place The Mermaid, the red-haired elf volunteered. She kept up the bland conversation as she let her eyes scan the clientele. Looking for… Looking for…

Anyone out of place.

Someone who didn't normally come here, like this priestess. But unlike her, someone unrefined, impolite, whose only serious distinguishing attribute was their money. Someone drunk on the pleasure of the very fact that they *could* come here.

"…So you've got a quest in the water town?" the elf asked.

"Uh-huh! Although, er, I'm not sure how much I can say about it."

Even as the elf looked, the talk continued. A little chatter while she searched.

It's a real help, in one way.

It would have been awfully strange, after all, for one of the harefolk-costumed servers to simply stand around doing nothing, staring at the customers. She certainly liked this better than walking around looking like she had nothing to do. She didn't know what had brought them together here, Fate or Chance, but she was grateful…

"Basically, we're looking for someone who was abducted."

"Kidnappers, huh?" The red-haired elf's ears laid back reflexively. "They're such scum. The lowest of the low."

"Er…?"

"Oh! Don't mind me. Sorry. Can't be having that!" The elf reproved herself, trying to pass the whole thing off with a smile. The tendency for her hatred of traffickers and kidnappers to appear at the drop of a hat was nothing more and nothing less than a vulnerability that could be exploited.

Gotta build up that karma.

Just like the girl, the one who was now looking at her with—was that suspicion? No, something closer to genuine concern. Maybe when this run was over, the elf could find her way to a temple of the Earth Mother.

She saw a man with a hard glint in his eye appear in a corner of the room, and she nodded briefly in his direction.

"Oh, it's starting!" the priestess said.

With a flourish, the lights in the casino were extinguished, darkness descending on the place. Instead, there was a spray of water from the tank on the stage, accompanied by an exclamation from the spectators.

The red-haired elf, totally ignoring all this, *tsk*'ed to herself and gave her feet an order. No one around her would have noticed the shadows by her toes writhing and slithering before making their way outside. And they certainly wouldn't have seen that the shadows were in the form of some kind of beast—no, they were much too enraptured by the spectacle onstage.

Now all she had to do was not take her eyes off the man. She couldn't relax, but the first act was coming to a close—

"Oh!"

"...!"

Thus when the priestess suddenly called out, the red-haired elf's shoulders shook with surprise. Had she been noticed? That was her first thought, but when she glanced at the priestess, she found the young woman looking somewhere she would never have predicted—namely, toward a distractingly scruffy-looking adventurer in a cheap metal helmet.

Did he come out of the inner room?

But, she thought, that would mean—but the red-haired elf threw the thought away. Between cats and runners, curiosity had probably claimed at least 50,000 lives in the Four-Cornered World.

"Um, I'm afraid I have to get going," the priestess said.

"Yeah? Stay safe out there."

Hence the elf wished the priestess good fortune as she stood to leave. A personal remark.

A runner who sped through the city's shadows and an adventurer who moved boldly across the hexes of the Four-Cornered World: Sometimes they might be at cross-purposes, but other times they might work together.

"I thought I saw your friend at work around here," the priestess said, adding wistfully that she would have liked to say hello, but he'd looked like he was busy.

The elf offered a crooked smile. "I'll give him your best."

"I'd appreciate that. Um, good-bye, then..." The priestess pattered several steps away, but then she turned back, her face flushed with concern, and asked, "Why are you all dressed like rabbits anyway?"

"Please," the elf said, covering her face, "don't ask."

CHAPTER 4

Flush Out the Mastermind!

"You learn anything?" High Elf Archer asked as she let the breeze blow pleasantly through her hair after it had made its journey across the field. The sky was clear and blue, except for a few white clouds that floated like dandelion fluff.

The adventurers were just outside the main gate of the water town, where they had reconvened after a night of gathering information.

"In the matter of this lanista," Lizard Priest said, his tail curling as he leaned toward High Elf Archer, "it seems he was rather in need of finances."

"Could be a rich vein of inquiry," Dwarf Shaman said—truly, a fitting turn of phrase for a dwarf. "But it don't mean quite what Scaly's implying. Seems our man was living beyond his means."

"Hmm?"

"Yeh *do* know that you can't grow a money tree by planting a coin in the ground, don't you?"

The elf's ears laid back: *How rude!* It would be uncouth at this point to go on about high elves' sense of economics.

Priestess, who was all too familiar with the elf's spending habits, could only offer a hollow chuckle. "So the question is where he was getting his money from, right?" she said, meanwhile glancing at Goblin Slayer, who remained steadfastly silent. "I suppose it would tabulate if he had some kind of side business..."

Based on her visit to the *ludus*, she had to say it didn't look like very easy work, although it seemed like the lanistas were being paid reasonably…

"If he *still* wasn't able to keep up with his own lifestyle, he must have really been living large," agreed High Elf Archer, who tended to buy toys and leave them in her room. She was smiling as if the grass beneath her feet was the most wonderful thing in the world; she looked like a delighted child as she walked around, kicking her feet through the field.

Such freedom, beauty so striking it could be a painting, was the special prerogative of the elves. There was no question but that this young woman was at her most lovely when she was out in nature, Priestess thought as she whispered to High Elf Archer, "How'd it go last night?"

"It went, I guess. We just chatted a bit," she replied, giggling in a way that made her long ears flutter.

She cast a significant look in the direction of Baturu, who was making the most of the open field. She no longer looked depressed the way she had the previous day, but her expression was still hard. The young centaur's lips were drawn, and she was gazing straight ahead—seemingly at the back of the grimy adventurer who went silently at the head of the group. Only the equine ears on her head, turned outward so that she would miss nothing, betrayed that she was listening to their conversation.

"…You think he sold my princess to get himself out of his money troubles?" she demanded.

"Only person who could tell us that for sure wound up with his head split open," Dwarf Shaman said. "Even if they'd brought a necromancer along, it wouldn't have helped much!" He laughed.

Then, too, good necromancers helped the souls of the dead return to the great cycle. The idea that resolving disputes in the mortal world helped spirits get over their attachment to their lives was just something the living told themselves.

"Here I thought Beard-cutter was taking us out to inspect the scene, but maybe not…"

"No," said the man who had brought them all out here and then hadn't spoken a word until this moment. "I'm looking for any sign of goblins."

The adventurers exchanged glances. One can imagine expressions that said, *Good grief* or *I knew it.* A feeling they all shared, a combination of exasperation, familiarity, affection, and fatigue.

Baturu, the one person who wasn't in on this reaction, gripped the hilt of her katana and veritably yelled, "But the quest is to find out where the princess went!"

"Exactly," Goblin Slayer said, his response brief and so sharp, it was almost painful. "The coachman, the motivation of the lanista's murderer—I don't believe these things are connected to what happened to Silver Blaze."

One might contend that that was a rather outrageous opinion. The adventurers looked at one another again; even Baturu seemed lost for what to say to this. Finally, High Elf Archer spoke up on behalf of them all, sounding prickly. "What exactly do you mean by that?"

"I mean what I said."

"We don't know what you meant by what you said; that's why we're asking!"

"Hmph." Goblin Slayer snorted quietly, then attempted to give new voice to his thoughts. "If nothing else, I don't believe that the fact that the centaur princess was abducted is connected to her disappearance from this town."

"It certainly would be quite roundabout," Lizard Priest said helpfully. He began to crook the fingers on his scaly hand, counting off: "First one tricks her into leaving her herd and sells her into competition, then kills her lanista and abducts her again."

When he put it that way, it did sound unlikely. Dwarf Shaman took a swig of wine to get his wits working, and then with alcohol-laden breath he said, "Even if you did want to negotiate for her twice, there must be a better way." Even that alleged dwarven sage would have figured out that much—although to be fair, that was just a story, and dwarves hated the way everybody thought they were all like him.

Priestess put a finger to her lips and, synthesizing what everyone else had said, remarked, "If you're going to make a plan, the simpler it is, the more likely it will work." She was a clever girl. Inexperienced, perhaps, but always ready to learn from those farther along the path. "If she had run away, she would have gone somewhere in the city or she would have returned to her people. Since she did neither, we know she was kidnapped..." That was the gift of education, that ability to think calmly through an idea—and find the answer. "I see. Yes, it's definitely goblins, then."

"Oh gods...," High Elf Archer groaned, looking incredulous.

Baturu pawed the grass angrily. "What are you saying?! My princess—!"

"A girl, alone, disappears outside of town. There are wandering goblins in the area," Goblin Slayer said, relentlessly laying out the facts. He concluded, "One may assume she was kidnapped by them."

§

The scene of the crime was so unremarkable that they would never have known where it was if they hadn't been told. Grass, mud: The rain had had its way with everything, and there was no longer any trace of the murder or the kidnapping.

That didn't stop Goblin Slayer from getting down on all fours and plunging a hand into the undergrowth. "If the archbishop is unaware of any goblins, I doubt the Adventurers Guild would have more information." The visits to the coliseum and the *ludus* had been invaluable in establishing the identity of Silver Blaze as the centaur princess, but for the purposes of his search, they held absolutely no more necessity than that. "That's why I tried the underworld. They had nothing to tell me about goblins, but I did hear about a suspicious sorcerer."

"A sorcerer, you say?" Dwarf Shaman asked.

"Yes," Goblin Slayer replied. "An immortal one, allegedly, who comes back to life no matter how many times he's killed. This person has shown up on the western frontier recently, or so they say."

"Immortal." Dwarf Shaman sniffed with no evident interest. "My eye."

There had never been an example of actual immortality in the whole history of the Four-Cornered World. Even the high elves eventually died. Neither was resurrection a simple matter. It was told of in one of the sagas, which claimed that a great hero had been resurrected by a miracle of the gods—a true miracle. But that was all. Immortality—such a thing didn't, couldn't exist. Those who claimed the undead were immortal were fools. The undead, after all, had risen again precisely because they were dead first.

"It wouldn't be the first time we've encountered goblins serving the likes of them."

If nothing else, a wandering tribe of goblins had appeared suddenly on the western frontier—and a girl had been abducted near a town. Someone else might have looked closer, investigated further, observed more before making a deduction. But for this man, everything came back to goblins.

"It's settled," Goblin Slayer said with conviction.

"...Is this really an urban adventure?" Priestess asked.

"Yeah, I don't think this counts anymore...," High Elf Archer said, covering her face and hoping to correct any misunderstanding Priestess might have about the nature of urban adventuring. She doubted it would help much, though. The girl was being progressively poisoned.

Freaking goblins! Again!

A pox upon Fate and Chance! (Far be it from a high elf to mutter anything so uncouth as *gygax!*)

"You don't even have any proof!" she retorted.

"Here it is," Goblin Slayer said, presenting his findings from the underbrush: He was holding up some animal droppings. Specifically, wolf dung—or even more precisely, those of a warg.

High Elf Archer frowned furiously, offering a very short and probably not terribly polite remark in the elegant language of her people. Priestess had no idea what she'd said; as far as she was concerned, it sounded as pretty as a song or a poem.

"...Why did no one notice this before?" Baturu demanded, trotting up and peering at the dung.

"Presumably because they were looking for a centaur's hoof marks or a person's footprints, not goblins."

"Then the princess really was kidnapped by goblins?"

"I don't know."

Even Baturu recognized the warg dung. So maybe this man, this scruffy man, wasn't simply blowing smoke. If he was—well, a high elf and this priestess would never have followed such a person.

"That's why I'm trying to find out. And then eventually, I will kill all the goblins."

Baturu had never seen the eyes hidden deep behind the visor of the metal helmet, couldn't imagine what they might look like—but she saw High Elf Archer intertwine her arms behind her head, accepting this declaration (with a certain amount of annoyance). And she saw Priestess grip her sounding staff firmly, gazing ahead to the horizon. Those things she understood.

"Is there a problem with that?" Goblin Slayer asked.

Baturu's response: "...No."

§

So it was that the adventurers found themselves in the field once more—on foot, with their packs on their backs. No cart or carriage would be flexible enough for their needs when they were wandering about the open plain, uncertain where they were going, so instead they found themselves using this most classic mode of transportation, their own two (or in Baturu's case, four) feet. A tradition among adventurers since they first put on their shining mail and began to explore.

The party went, advancing over the grid and hexes of the Four-Cornered World.

"...Where exactly are we going?"

"We're looking for goblins."

The exchange between Baturu and Goblin Slayer was not so much one of frustration met with displeasure as simply a question met with an answer.

The sunlight that poured down uninterrupted upon the field was almost as brutal as that in the desert. At least they didn't have the reflected heat of the sand.

Brutal it might be, but for adventurers, it was not hard going. Elves, dwarves, and even lizardmen were not really built for walking long distances—the fact that they could make their way across the grass, vigilant all the while, was one of the gifts of their long experience.

In a situation like this, it was humans who held the overwhelming advantage. They might sweat, they might breathe hard, but they could walk along silently. In terms of pure speed or strength, they might not compare to other people, but—

"They say humans never give up. But I guess maybe they take a break every once in a while," High Elf Archer said, a bit exasperated.

But she chuckled, watching Priestess from behind as the young woman worked forward in front of her. She looked so delicate and fragile, yet here she was. It made High Elf Archer happy and sad at the same time. At least Priestess was starting to understand her "older sister's" word of warning.

"...You okay?" Priestess asked, trying to cover for herself by turning to Baturu beside her.

"No problem...at all...," the centaur said through gritted teeth. She came from a nomadic people; a bit of walking was nothing new to her—but a steady march of almost ten *li* was something else again. The handful of brief breaks they'd taken along the way weren't enough to outweigh the mounting fatigue.

"Well, best we not overdo it. Gotta be ready to fight if we need to." The real work was yet to come, as Dwarf Shaman well knew. He held something out to Baturu—a dried apricot, sitting in his weathered palm. Now, where had he gotten that?

"Thanks..."

"Don't mention it!"

Baturu's gaze, prickly to begin with, had softened over their days of working together. Or maybe she really was feeling just that weak—whatever the case, she took the fruit gratefully.

"Ooh! Me too, me too!" High Elf Archer exclaimed.

"What are ya, a kid?" Dwarf Shaman snapped.

The elf objected that there was no reason to object, and he obligingly gave her some apricot, while he himself took a swig of his wine.

The sun would soon pass over their heads and begin its descent toward the horizon. Lizard Priest, who had been studying its path through the sky, called out to their van, "Milord Goblin Slayer, I daresay collapsing from exhaustion here will do us no good!"

"Mm," said Goblin Slayer, coming to a halt.

Priestess pulled up short beside him, her staff jangling in her hands. "Are we going to make camp?"

"It seems to be the time."

Priestess had become more accustomed to travel than she would ever have imagined during her days at the temple. The water town, the royal capital, the snowy mountain, the village of the elves, the desert, the northern sea, and many a dungeon and ancient ruin—she had been to them all. But among those experiences…

I hardly ever just walk through the open field!

What a strange thought. She smiled; what an odd thing to realize at this moment. And yet, despite this lack of experience with the field proper, somewhere along the line she'd picked up the instinct to start pitching camp before it got dark.

What about him? she wondered. Had Goblin Slayer experienced many adventures like this?

Still not knowing the answer, a mumble escaped Priestess: "We never did find the goblins."

"It will work out," Goblin Slayer said, looking across the sea of green, to each of the four corners in turn. He said quietly, "Eventually, they will come to us."

§

In due course, night came. The moons rose in the sky, shimmering red and green, while on the ground, light came from the crackling bonfire. Each of the adventurers did what they thought was best, resting themselves or keeping watch. The spell casters slept while the warrior and the ranger were charged with standing guard. High Elf Archer took the first watch, saying she wanted to be able to sleep once she turned in, rather than being woken up in the middle of the night.

It was another phase of another adventure, a perfectly ordinary occurrence repeated many a time across the Four-Cornered World. It was an unfamiliar situation, however, for those who were not adventurers. Baturu, with her horselike body, shifted uncomfortably on top of the blanket that had been laid out in place of a bed for her.

It was natural, therefore, that *she* would approach the kneeling centaur. "Can't sleep?" Priestess asked, quietly so as not to disturb her friend on guard.

"........" There was a very long silence, after which Baturu finally replied, "No... Among my *ulus*, my people, we always put up tents under which we would sleep."

"I think tents would be a little much for us to carry..."

"I don't mean of the kind adventurers use. Our *gers* are our houses." Baturu smiled ever so slightly. She explained that a post was erected in the center of the tent, a roof constructed, the entire thing surrounded with a frame and then covered in cloth. "It has a proper roof and a proper door. Furniture too. Even a stove."

"A stove...!" Priestess found herself blinking. She'd never seen a tent like that. They must be very large. And how could you carry a stove around? She couldn't imagine it.

Baturu smiled again at Priestess's childlike amazement and looked up at the sky. "That's why I find it...difficult to relax under the stars."

"Me too. My heart wouldn't stop pounding the first time." Priestess drew her knees into her chest, edging closer to Baturu.

When had her first time camping out been? Maybe about when they had all gone to the ancient ruins?

The wind across the plain was cold, and the chill was only deepened by the gleam of the moons and stars. But the centaur's body was warm, Priestess thought, letting out a contented breath. Then she finally remembered that she had brought over the waterskin. "Would you like a drink?"

"Mn... Yes, please."

Baturu's ears drooped, and she took the canteen with surprising willingness. Before she put any of it into her mouth, she poured a few drops on the middle finger of her right hand. She flung the droplets to the sky, to the earth, and only then did she drink lustily.

"What's that?" Priestess asked. She'd seen Baturu make a similar gesture before they started eating.

"Hmm," Baturu replied and thought for a second. "An act of

gratitude, I suppose you could say. To the heavens and the earth." She smiled shyly, as if struggling a little to come up with a good summary. "It's a custom of ours. Easier to do than to explain."

"Ah…"

So it was for Baturu like prayer was for her, Priestess reflected with a nod. Ultimately, that was how faith was. Not having it would be like not breathing—she wouldn't be able to think, wouldn't even survive.

At least, that's the ideal, Priestess thought. Not that she'd gotten anywhere near it.

"Mm…," Baturu grunted, holding the waterskin out to Priestess.

"Oh, um," Priestess began, then managed, "thank you very… much?" as she accepted the canteen.

"I don't think you have to thank me. It's yours."

"… That's right."

Baturu chuckled—Priestess was hopeless!—and Priestess scratched her cheek with embarrassment. For some reason, though, she didn't find herself too upset at having her little gaffe pointed out.

She took a swallow of the water, which was mixed with some wine. *Glug, glug.* Baturu studied Priestess's face in the light from the moons, stars, and fire. "Why did you become an adventurer?" she asked, her question coming neatly in between crackles from the fire.

"Why…?"

"It doesn't make sense to me. Not why my older sister would leave, nor why a princess would go to a city."

They were the words of one who had been left behind. Priestess had never heard anything quite like them.

"If it's fighting she wants, there are battles. We have our wars. There's glory to be won!" She had friends; she had a family. She had her daily work and her joys and sorrows. They might move frequently from place to place, yet where she *lived* had never changed. "The plain is a good place," Baturu said, looking out at the dark ocean of grass that extended endlessly under the night sky. Whenever the wind blew, a wave would pass through it, accompanied by a susurration like the whispering of the sea. "This is my homeland. Was it not enough for her?"

"Well…"

"Last night, I heard that even your elf princess left her home." Baturu was posing a question to Priestess, and yet, it was almost more like she was talking to herself. "Is it…really that bad?"

"I'm…not sure," Priestess said softly, pressing her cheek into her knees. "I'm no princess, and I'm not your sister."

"…You're right. Of course not."

Baturu's voice seemed a touch gentler. Maybe it was because Priestess hadn't said it was because she wasn't a centaur. Or perhaps because she hadn't expressed some misplaced sympathy or fellow feeling. Even Priestess couldn't be sure.

"But the reason we are continuing this adventure is because…"

Because we understand?

Could she say that? Priestess hugged her knees and whispered the words. She wasn't an accomplished enough adventurer to claim she understood. There were others more experienced than she. Everyone who made up her party.

What about Goblin Slayer?

What about him? Why had he chosen this path he had walked, this road that had brought him to this point? She didn't know.

She knew why he kept killing goblins. He believed it was what he had to do.

Priestess believed the same.

Protect, heal, save. The teachings of the Earth Mother, which had been inculcated into her since she was little, and which stood as guideposts for her life.

Why was she an adventurer, then?

There was one answer.

It had to be—

"Because I want to go on adventures."

That was the only reason.

"You want to go on…?" Now it was Baturu's turn to blink in surprise.

Priestess was sure her long-eared friend, standing guard, must be able to hear them, and that was a little embarrassing—but there was no hesitation when she spoke. "I mean, you never have any idea what's going to happen!"

She had never even dreamed she might fight a dragon. Never thought she might make friends with a *húsfreya* on the northern sea. Or that she would meet precious friends like High Elf Archer, or Female Merchant, or King's Sister (even if she had gotten awfully annoyed at the royal sibling the first time they'd met).

It wasn't all good things—there had been many things that were bad, even heartbreaking. Where would she be now if she'd been able to keep traveling with her very first party? Even now, the question caused a hot prickle in her chest every time it crossed her mind. And yet, if she'd stopped adventuring then…

"I wouldn't be talking with a centaur princess, would I?"

"…I am not a princess," Baturu said after a moment.

"To me, you look every bit as noble as one."

She was a young lady from a good martial family of the centaur people. In human terms, that would make her something like the distinguished daughter of a knight's lineage.

That's princess enough for me, certainly, Priestess thought. How different from herself, raised in a temple orphanage, never so much as knowing her parents' faces. Although to be fair, only when she was extremely young had she ever believed her situation unfortunate.

The fact that someone like her was here, with so many friends and acquaintances, was thanks to adventures.

"Please don't tease me," Baturu said, her ears laying back on her head. Her lips were pursed, but maybe the red in her cheeks was from the reflection of the fire?

"Hee-hee! I'm not teasing you."

"You are! I'm sure you are…! I can see it in your face," Baturu asserted, glowering.

Priestess only giggled. "I promise I'm not."

They should really get some sleep, but here she was, chatting the night away with a friend. Some might deride this as lack of vigilance or arrogance—but an adventure that didn't have at least one moment like this was hardly an adventure at all. A simple, innocent chat, that's what this was.

But there were those in the Four-Cornered World who would not permit even such simple indulgences.

High Elf Archer was the first to notice them. "Mn...," she grunted, her ears twitching; then she quickly reached for her bow.

Their approach could never fail to escape Goblin Slayer. "...Goblins?" he asked, getting to his feet with a movement that was not particularly agile but was very practiced.

High Elf Archer nodded to Goblin Slayer as he checked to make sure the hasps of his equipment were tight. "Well, this sucks."

"All right."

"No, it's all *wrong*!"

"I agree."

High Elf Archer snorted. The worst part was that he meant it.

Priestess, who had already grasped the situation, was busy waking up the spell casters.

"Hrm...?" Dwarf Shaman grunted as she shook him out of a dream.

"I think there are enemies...!" she said.

"Well! Well now!" Lizard Priest exclaimed, catching the whiff of battle. The way his whole great body shook as he arose was like a dragon getting to its feet. "My goodness, but the plain does get cold at night. Have you anything to warm the blood?"

"If by that you mean wine, yes, I have some," Priestess said with a giggle, smiling with only a hint of anxiety.

Even in battle, it was always good to have a little something in reserve—at least enough for some friendly banter. Maybe she couldn't do what her knight friend had done, but she could at least try to imitate her.

"How many of 'em, Long Ears?"

"The wargs' howling is making it tough to tell..." Dwarf Shaman was digging through his bag of catalysts even as he stood up, while High Elf Archer flicked her ears and tried answering the question he'd pelted to her over the grass. "More than three of them, I think? And definitely less than ten."

"Can't yeh even count that high?" Dwarf Shaman said.

This was followed by a "shut up, dwarf!" But understandably, both of them spoke in hushed tones.

The stink of beasts came to them on the wind, a combination of filth and dirt.

"I suppose you knew this would happen," Lizard Priest said, squeezing some wine out of the canteen.

"I suspected," Goblin Slayer replied with a nod. Behind his visor, his eye shone across the field, across the ocean of grass, a fiery shimmer like the gaze of a wild animal.

To the enemy, they must have looked like nothing more than idiots stupid enough to camp out in the open field.

"These are foolish enough to attack a wagon in broad daylight," Goblin Slayer noted. "They would never have missed a campfire burning at night."

"I can't believe you," High Elf Archer said with a scowl. "You mean we were the *bait*?"

"Yes."

"Unbelievable..."

"But there is good news," Goblin Slayer said. "They don't appear to have enough yet."

Whether they were looking for living sacrifices, workers, or *amusements*, one centaur evidently wasn't enough to fill their needs. If the enemy hadn't yet achieved their objective, it meant there was a chance Silver Blaze was still alive. And since that chance wasn't zero, it had become more than one. Good news.

"...What should I do?" Baturu asked. She was in her full armor, her sword in her hand. She might not be accustomed to adventures, but she knew how to fight. She was nervous, but not scared.

"Save your strength," said Goblin Slayer, who had drawn his own sword of a strange length. "There's something I'll need you to do."

"And what's that...?"

"I'll tell you when the time comes."

With that, the conversation ceased. It wasn't that they had sensed any aura, or murderous intent, or whatever you wanted to call it—but long experience had given them a feeling for what would happen and when.

There was an instant as the goblins closed the distance to their prey. The adventurers stood at the ready, one on each side of the fire. From the darkness came a powerful stench. A rustling of the grass.

The rustling was not caused by the wind. It was someone, something. Priestess swallowed, just a little, and then the enemy was upon them.

"GROORGB!!!!"

Wild goblins came leaping out of the tall grass.

§

"WAROOGB?!"

It's easy enough to respond to something you've completely anticipated. Goblin Slayer dove underneath the leaping warg, piercing it through the heart. His blade, stabbing between its bones, might have killed the creature, but it didn't kill its momentum. He allowed the undiminished speed of the animal's body, tumbling behind him, to enable him to draw out his sword.

"That's one…!"

"GBBROG?!"

He jumped atop the goblin, who tumbled off the dead warg, driving his sword backhanded into the monster's eyeball. The goblin gave a few pathetic spasms, but his soul was no longer in this world.

"How many?" Goblin Slayer asked.

"I'd say eight more!" High Elf Archer called even as she pulled back the arrow in her bow. It went scudding across the ground, but just as it vanished into the darkness of some undergrowth, it bounced upward.

"WARG?!"

"GBBOG?!?!"

Two screams. The single shot had pierced the mount and its rider directly through their chins. High Elf Archer licked her lips. "I would say sixteen altogether, fourteen left!"

"All right…!"

The adventurers surrounded the camp on all four sides, with Priestess and Baturu in the middle, by the fire. As far as the goblins were concerned, however, they still vastly outnumbered the foe. They would overwhelm and crush them. It was the only idea they had.

Thus, they were not at all coordinated. Each was desperate to be the first, plunging ahead, leaving his stupider comrades behind. Or they might let their idiotic companions push forward, using them as cannon fodder while they, the smart ones, held back to grab the spoils.

The goblins came flying at the adventurers, usually with one of these two self-centered thoughts in their heads.

"I'm holding off on miracles for now!" Priestess said, casting a look in each of the four directions and grasping her staff as she stood ready beside the fire. It was agonizing not to be able to see in the dark, but adventures were all about differing roles. At that moment, holding station with Baturu was the right thing to do.

"If they get too close, I'll be counting on you," Priestess said.

"...Right," responded the centaur, nodding with a hint of tension. "Just leave it to me."

"I'm doing everything I can to roll out the welcome mat with my arrows," High Elf Archer said, unleashing a literal hail of bolts even as she spoke. "But riders are the worst if they get past you!" She scowled.

"Mayhap it's time for a little spell, then?" Dwarf Shaman said. He reached into his bag and came up with a small jar of oil. Without a second thought, he flung it on the field. *"Fairies, fairies, never tarry—what you forgot, I give back fairly! I don't need cash, but make me merry!"*

No sooner had he intoned the incantation than behold! Oil flowed endlessly from the jar. Soon the fragrant stuff was everywhere around the field, a greasy flicker in the dark.

"GOROGGB?!?!"

"WAGGRG?!"

The goblins came charging heedlessly on, only to be unhorsed—er, undogged. The unlucky ones fell headfirst, dying as their necks bent in unnatural directions. The relatively fortunate goblins tried to get their feet under them but without much success as they slipped and slid on the oily ground.

"They claim that's supposed to be healing oil," Dwarf Shaman said, flipping a coin toward the jar to stop the oil from flowing. The instant the coin hit the ground, amazingly, the flow of oil dried up.

"I wish I could set fire to it," said Goblin Slayer.

"Oh, *please* don't!" High Elf Archer groaned.

As the goblins flopped around as if they were drowning, they were pierced by Goblin Slayer's dagger or High Elf Archer's arrows.

There were a few lucky ones, however, who managed to get across the sea of oil or simply to avoid it entirely—or was it the intelligence of their wargs at work? The one thing that seemed certain was that it was not the bequest of any special goblin skill.

One warg was very unlucky: He had the misfortune to leap at Lizard Priest.

"I must applaud your spirit!"

"WARGGGGG…?!"

The creature's fangs went for his throat, but they didn't close. Instead, they found themselves caught by two scaly hands and wrenched apart, teeth and all.

"GBBB…?! GOROGBB?!?!"

The goblin in the saddle took a few jabs with a rusty spear, but it was nothing close to enough to bother Lizard Priest, who cried, "Eeeey-aahhh!" and tore the warg in two before it could make another sound. Fur and flesh were rent with a spray of blood, internal organs scattering everywhere.

"GROOGB! GOBBGRGBB!!" The goblin who went tumbling through the middle of all this howled uncomprehendingly, 80 percent out of anger at his warg, 20 percent in mockery of the adventurer who had failed to kill him.

"You're mine!"

"GOROGB?!?!"

Thus he left himself open to something that was neither of them: Baturu, splitting his skull like firewood with her katana. Brains and blood poured out of his head as Baturu resumed a ready posture. From her lips could be heard a murmur: "Truly astonishing…"

"Ha-ha-ha! Do you mean my strength? Or perhaps our shaman's little tricks?"

"Both!"

"Ha-ha-ha!" Lizard Priest's jolly laughter echoed across the dark field. It sounded like the roaring of a dragon and was enough to frighten the wargs—but not the goblins. The wargs had never thought of the goblins as their masters and were indeed smarter than they were.

"WARG! WWAAAAAARG!!"

"WARGGGGG!!!"

Without hesitation, they shook off their riders and literally turned tail and ran across the open field. That left only a handful of goblins in the grass. And half of them were flopping around in the oil.

"...Hrmph," Goblin Slayer grunted as he calmly stabbed one of the floppers to death. "I never thought a battle with goblins in an open field would be this easy."

"What did you expect? There's not many of them," High Elf Archer said.

It felt like a waste to use her arrows on them now. Instead, she drew an obsidian dagger and went about slitting their throats, though she frowned as she did so. No matter how often she did it, she never got used to this businesslike way of killing. At least this time, it was the result of a proper battle.

"GOORGB...!!"

The battle might have been over, but that didn't mean she would miss it as one of the oily goblins managed to clamber to his feet.

These goblins! They don't know when to give up...!

High Elf Archer gave an unladylike "tsk" and quickly swapped her dagger for her bow.

"Don't kill him," Goblin Slayer said sharply. "Aim for a nonvital point."

"What?" High Elf Archer cried disbelievingly as she loosed the arrow—but even so, the shot went right where she wanted it to.

"GOBG?!?!"

The creature yowled and fell to the ground with an arrow in his shoulder, then immediately got up and began to run. The high elf's archery was so sublime that it could have passed for a magic spell.

It would never cross the goblin's mind that he had been *allowed* to live. No, the stupid elf had missed her shot! It was of some annoyance to High Elf Archer that he would be alive to gloat.

"I think I remember you saying something like that once before, Orcbolg..."

Before. Funny thing to hear a high elf say, Priestess thought with a smile. Baturu looked at her questioningly, whereupon she coughed and said, "Nothing." Then she began making sure that all the goblins around them were really finished—she'd been surprised once by a goblin merely playing dead—but she found time to ask, "Going to pursue him?"

"Yes. I expect he'll run straight to his nest for help. He won't think about anything else." Goblin Slayer nodded, then turned to High Elf Archer and Baturu. "I want the two of you to go after him. But don't let him notice you."

High Elf Archer blinked, and with one long, pale finger, she pointed to herself and then to the centaur. "Two of us?" she asked.

"A lookout and a messenger. A high elf should be able to see in the dark. A centaur can run quickly." The cheap metal helmet turned to look at Baturu, and to the centaur, it seemed he was saying: *You can do that, yes?* "I want you to find out where they're hiding. Silver Blaze may be there."

"...!" With a sharp intake of breath, Baturu bit her lip hard and nodded. "All right...!"

"Okay, let's go!" High Elf Archer gently smacked Baturu on what amounted to her flank—and then the two of them were off, as quick as the wind, racing after the goblin.

Needless to say, a centaur's speed is without equal. Even a high elf can't keep up with one on open ground. But if the centaur is going slowly enough to avoid raising hoofbeats, that's another matter—or if she's deliberately going at the elf's pace.

It was certainly the latter, Priestess figured as she watched them disappear.

"If nothing else, we've confirmed the foe is here," Lizard Priest said, slapping the ground with his tail to shake off some of the blood that had spattered on him. "Enough that one centaur is not going to satisfy them. The little monsters must be starving and thirsty."

"Yes." Goblin Slayer's helmet nodded slowly up and down. That was how goblins were.

He'd expected that a battle against goblins in the open field would be more difficult. He didn't think he would lose, but he'd thought it would take more time. It was exceptionally good fortune that they had cleaned up these creatures as quickly as they had.

"However, we did use up a spell. We should rest until the girls come back."

"Don't think she'll just go charging in?" Dwarf Shaman said, but his tone made it clear that he didn't believe she would. He collected the jar he'd thrown down, carefully wiping it off before placing it back in his pouch. Strangely enough, the coin he'd tossed was nowhere to be seen.

"She won't," Goblin Slayer said.

"Fair enough. I s'pose she does have Long Ears with 'er."

"Mm." The metal helmet nodded, and above his beard, the dwarf's eyes twinkled. It was something of an open secret that as disinterested as this man could seem, he put a surprising amount of faith in his comrades. The fact that he had begun to show it outwardly, even this tiny bit…

If that tomboy knew about it, she'd only get on her high horse.

So Dwarf Shaman decided to keep quiet about it and savor it as a side dish to his wine. Speaking of which, he grabbed the drink he kept at his hip and drank lustily in honor of their triumph in battle. Surprising? Between a dwarf who hasn't had a drink and one who has, the second is far more likely to prevail in combat.

"What's more," Goblin Slayer said, "doesn't it feel bad to not be entrusted with anything?"

Priestess blinked. The words seemed to be directed at her. They invoked something she'd said to him long ago, on a mountain in winter.

"Yes!" she replied, puffing out her flat chest and grinning. "That's right!"

§

It was nearly dawn when Goblin Slayer caught the sound of hooves.

"How does it look?" he asked.

The spell casters were busy resting, notably Dwarf Shaman, who sat meditating in a lotus posture. The man who crouched, watching over them, could have been taken for a dilapidated suit of armor. It was hard even to tell whether he was awake or asleep—until the armor spoke.

Baturu goggled at the scene for a second as she arrived—or perhaps it was a look of tension at the battle that must be coming. "We found them," she said in a hard voice. "I'll take you to them. This way."

It wasn't far. With Baturu leading, the party moved quickly over the field in the gray light of dawn. Waves of purplish light rolled by, accompanied by the whispering of the grass as they moved.

They did not use torches. Nighttime might be the goblins' friend, but there was no need to deliberately give away their position. After all, the open field was not the inside of a cave.

Yaaawwwn.

How could a yawn escape Priestess at a time like this? She'd had a good rest…albeit a short one. Dwarf Shaman looked unbothered—maybe it was a difference in how much they had trained. As for Lizard Priest—well, she didn't exactly know what he looked like when he was tired.

Suddenly, Priestess found herself looking at the man in the grimy leather armor following silently behind Baturu. He hadn't slept at all, yet his movements seemed as sharp as ever. "…Are you all right?" she asked.

"It's no problem," he said. "I can sleep with one eye open."

Priestess wasn't even sure if he was joking or not.

"Pick up the pace, Orcbolg," High Elf Archer called suddenly from among the sea of grass.

"Ah," he said.

Maybe it was true that the elves were close to the rheas, who were said to be spirits of the grass and fields, for Priestess could barely pick High Elf Archer out on the plain. She blended that well into the overgrowth.

"Sorry. I thought I was leading us fairly quickly…" Baturu was despondent, her ears drooping.

"I didn't mean you," High Elf Archer said with a slight smile. Her eyes never left the distance.

"Where are they?" Goblin Slayer asked.

"You can see it."

As dawn began to break over the horizon, they could see it rising before them: a dark, triangular shape. It made Priestess think of the ancient tomb of the king spoken of in the desert country. Whatever it was, it didn't look natural—but who would build something like that in an open field like this? It was made of countless rocks piled atop one another so that it seemed like a tiny mountain.

"What is that?" she asked.

"An *obo*," Baturu replied. "A sacred heap of stones. Passersby pile stones as they go, praying for a safe journey. Over hundreds or thousands of years, the pile grows."

"Thousands of years..."

"Proof that centaurs have been here."

Priestess blinked, then took a fresh, close look at the heap. Maybe it had been a small hill to begin with—or a monolith. Whatever it was, people crossing this plain had stopped there. The pile of stones, placed one by one on top of each other, was like a pile of the passing centaurs' thoughts and hopes.

"We sometimes call them tobacco stones," Baturu said with a smile. "Because they resemble the tobacco the rheas smoke."

But at the moment, the pile was nothing so innocent. Hideous creatures of Chaos could be seen all around it. Creatures with green skin and golden eyes that looked spitefully up at the incoming sun.

Goblins.

They were there. At least ten or twenty, surrounding the stones. The way the shadows shifted suggested there must be more among the rocks.

With a sound of battle lust that rumbled from within his great jaws, Lizard Priest smiled, baring his fangs. "Gracious me, but these little devils know no respect, do they?"

"Or the spell caster controllin' 'em is a blasphemer, more like," Dwarf Shaman said angrily, upset that they were trying to pollute the wind, which was the gift of the Trade God, the patron saint of travelers. "So, Long Ears. You know where this alleged immortal sorcerer or whoever is?"

"On the highest point, I suspect. The very top of the mountain." The elf's ears twitched, bobbing up and down. "Can't you hear it? Some sort of weird voice or...singing."

Priestess tried to listen. She could just make out something on the wind, a faint hum, difficult to describe and of uncertain meaning.

Words that cursed the gods, cursed the world, and wished for catastrophe upon all the four corners.

Priestess felt something cold pierce the very center of her being, her small form seeming to freeze. It was the same way she felt when she saw the goblins with their hideous laughter. This was the archetypal prayer of beings who thought only and ever of themselves. In other words…

"…It's a ritual, isn't it?" Priestess said.

"It means we're not too late," was Goblin Slayer's brusque assessment.

He had no interest at all in what kind of ritual this undying sorcerer or whoever might be conducting. What mattered to him was that this person was using goblins. And the fact that if the ritual was still ongoing, then the sacrifice would still be alive.

Very well: His thoughts moved on to the next step.

How to kill them.

He crouched in the underbrush, studying the goblins in the morning light. "Can you snipe them?" he asked.

"If my arrows can reach them," High Elf Archer said, shrugging. The elves shot their bows not with skill, nor with the eye, but with the spirit. She was indicating that hitting a distant target as such was no challenge at all. Not the wind, nor the distance, nor the difference in height could forestall a high elf's arrow. But that didn't mean there would be no problems here. "That princess or whoever is supposed to be around, right? I'm a little concerned they might try to use her as a shield."

Or consider the possibility that the targets might be wearing missile-deflection charms.

If one didn't fear the results of a critical fumble, then it was no adventure. But an adventurer who didn't consider the possible consequences of such a failure would not live long. Fate and Chance ever attended these endeavors.

Goblin Slayer grunted softly. "What do you think?"

"Terrain that is easy to defend and difficult to attack," said Lizard Priest. If one were to ask which people was the most versed in tactics and strategy in the Four-Cornered World, the answer would have to be the lizardmen. Though a monk, Lizard Priest was still one of their number, and his eye upon the tobacco rock was perceptive. "However, I believe their actual defensive measures are rather scant."

"You think so?" Priestess asked, cocking her head.

"For one thing, there don't appear to be any fortifications," Lizard Priest replied, nodding. With one sharp claw, he began to scratch a simple diagram in the earth, a large circle, surrounded by a panoply of little dots on each side. "If one had, say, twenty soldiers and divided them evenly, it would be five to a side. In terms of fighting strength..."

"It's about even," Priestess concluded, nodding seriously.

It was like a game of hnefatafl. During her games, Priestess had been charged with the defending side, and she knew how difficult it had been to hold off the attackers and allow her king to escape.

Right now, the enemy's objective was to perform a ritual atop the tobacco stone. In other words, if they could cause the defenders to even think about fleeing, it would mean the enemy's objective had been neutralized. And that meant...

"This situation might just be a little better for us than I'd realized." Clearly, Priestess had soaked up experience like a sponge, one thing after another. Lizard Priest felt that within this young, weak, modest girl, he had spotted a dragon—and there was no more wonderful thing than that.

"If we press forward, it will be easy enough to get out. The only question is how to climb the hill with the greatest rapidity."

"Hrm..." came the soft grunt from under the helmet. "How are your spells?"

"Just fine," replied Dwarf Shaman, who had had more than enough rest to get back the one spell he'd used. He patted the bag at his side. "Plenty of catalysts, too."

So they were well supplied with magical resources. The enemies were goblins. Standard stuff. Much as he disliked fighting in the open field.

Still, it is better than having to fight alone.

"I can consider you part of our number, yes?" Goblin Slayer asked in the middle of his considerations. He was speaking to Baturu.

She grasped the scabbard of her katana and pursed her lips. "*Now* you ask?" It almost sounded like bravado, somewhere between acting tough and putting on a show. Yet there was no doubt in her eyes; she held the grimy metal helmet fast in her gaze. "I've come this far to rescue the princess."

Goblin Slayer nodded. Good. That was fine, then.

"Prepare a Dragontooth Warrior. Will need all the help we can get," he said.

"Of course. Very good!" Lizard Priest responded immediately. He dug out several dragon fangs, sharp and terrible, from his bag and cast them up on the ground. *"O horns and claws of our father, iguanodon, thy four limbs, become two legs to walk upon the earth!"*

The fangs began to bubble and swell, puffing up as they knitted into bones until a warrior stood upon the ground before them.

"Well...well, now!" Baturu said, her eyes widening at the power of the nagas. "That's amazing."

"Hee-hee!" For some reason, High Elf Archer chuckled, puffing out her modest chest. "Cool, right?"

"What're yeh so pleased about, y'anvil?" Dwarf Shaman grumbled, sending the archer from the heights of satisfaction directly to "what'd you say?!"

They were off and running. They kept their voices down, but the argument proceeded as usual. Priestess could only giggle at Baturu's evident confusion. It was okay. This actually meant there was no problem. If you could conduct yourself this way, it meant the adventure would go well.

"All right, Goblin Slayer, sir. Shall we get started?" Priestess asked.

"Yes. At the moment, it is their twilight. The guard will be more lax than in the middle of the night." He added: "Also, even an immortal sorcerer will die if you push them from a high enough hill."

§

"Hmph."

Speaking of that sorcerer, he sensed something; it felt like a fly had darted past his face. On a whim, he looked up at the dawn sky, the color of dried blood.

Well, maybe it wasn't quite accurate to say "he" looked up. Ultimate beings had no need of such things as gender.

A fly was of little concern to the ritual that would take him to that point. Still, accidents happened sometimes—a single fly could cause a complicated Gate spell to go awry. The whole fact that the sorcerer paid even the slightest attention to it was a sign of his seriousness, his commitment.

"...What is it?" he said, taking a breath to bring his consciousness back from the depths of meditation.

From the sacred hill known as a tobacco stone, he rose and looked out. Among the irregular arrangement of the rocks, shadows writhed and squirmed chaotically, all the way to the foot of the mountain. The goblin horde, with whom the sorcerer had joined forces in contravention of every human moral, was beneath the sorcerer's contempt. Stupid and ignorant—yet proud and arrogant. Useless, incompetent fools. Everything the sorcerer disdained was there before him. For that reason, he could not have cared less what happened to the goblins who served him. It simply held no interest for him. Much as the sorcerer himself held scant interest for anyone else in the Four-Cornered World.

"......How dare she look at me that way?"

There was only one thing that displeased the sorcerer: the girl, currently placed as the offering in the middle of the magical diagram the sorcerer had carved.

She was a centaur. Her clothes had been violently ripped away so that now every inch of her naked skin was exposed to the wind.

And yet, the goblins' taunts, their cruel stares, couldn't humiliate this young woman. For her lovely curves and her womanliness were not the only things she had. Somewhere within, beneath the ripples that swept across her body with each breath, was a source of life that they could not snuff out. Her eyes were as bright and clear as a porcelain doll's, and her chestnut hair was so rich that it seemed to glow gold even in the misty predawn light.

Above all, there was the silver comet that streaked through her hair.

Anyone would have done, the sorcerer thought.

And yet, only she would do. If he could take the radiance of her life in his hands, then all would go well.

He didn't know her name, nor who she was—but she was not looking at the sorcerer. Her eyes were pointed in his direction, true—but they did not perceive him.

"Do you, too, mock me?" the sorcerer—the one who had achieved immortality—grumbled darkly.

"____"

There was no answer. Perhaps the centaur girl didn't wish to answer.

He gave her another good glare, then harrumphed. He spared her a little snort. "Well, it matters not. Eventually you will live within me, and you will understand, whether you wish to or not."

Before, when he had said he would live a hundred, a thousand years, everyone had laughed at him—but they were all in the ground now. None was left who remembered the name of the boy who had been ridiculed at the Sages Academy.

Then there were the adventurers who had come to kill him, claiming that there was no such thing as eternal life. Their names were forgotten, too, and had been for a very long time. They became merely one more part of *his* story, one more thing he had dealt with in his long and terrible career. Nearly unworthy of his notice—but even so, he felt some pleasure at the outcome. It was always nice to know that his value was rising.

It didn't matter what happened to anyone else. For example, who cared if the goblins were screaming and yammering at that moment?

"Hoh..."

He had been right: There was a fly. He picked up his staff and gazed down at the clamoring goblins. They gibbered uselessly, grabbing their weapons and running around. One particular corner of the rocky hill seemed to be the source of the commotion.

Damnable fools.

That was the sorcerer's estimation of any assassin who would come to try to take his life. There were so many who had sought to forestall his attempts at eternal life, out of jealousy or perhaps ignorance. No doubt more such had come, he figured. What fools these adventurers were!

Well, let the goblins tear them apart and eat their innards. The women might find their wombs defiled first, but in the long run, they would meet the same fate as the men, in a goblin stewpot. It was no real loss. Everyone got snake eyes eventually—it just hadn't happened on the first roll for them.

And I, I will use all of it to ascend ever higher, the sorcerer thought.

"Have at me, adventurers!"

Clutching his staff, he stood imperiously above the repugnant intruders, looking down at them. The wind that blew through the pre-dawn air carried the stench of death. He took a deep breath, filling his lungs with it, and, not caring that there was no one to hear his pronouncement, said: "I think I'll entertain myself with you for a while!"

He didn't know yet that the adventurers were coming from behind him.

§

"ARGOOOOOOOO!!!" the Dragontooth Warrior howled as it leaped upon the goblins.

Meanwhile, the adventurers worked their way quickly around the other side of the tobacco stone. "For the little devils are like a school of fish, you see," Lizard Priest said, crouching so low that he was almost on all fours as he sped along. It was the only way he could hope to even remotely hide his huge frame in the underbrush. "Toss them a morsel and they go rushing to it."

Even if there was some grander individual present, they could take control but not command.

And indeed, the goblins were busy flocking to the morsel—the enemy—that had been provided to them.

"GOROGB?!?!"

"GOROG! GBBROBGBGR!!"

It was unclear whether they were driven by fear of the goblins who were shouting importantly or simple self-interest.

"Not all of them," Goblin Slayer said. He concluded, however, that it didn't matter. "I am going to kill all the goblins."

It made no special difference to him why that particular goblin happened to be around the back of the tobacco stone. The monster was lolling there with a rusty spear in his hand, even letting out a yawn. A bud-tipped bolt through the brain put an end to his boredom.

"Go—I'll cover you!" High Elf Archer called as the goblin toppled to the ground without a sound.

Goblin Slayer and Lizard Priest didn't respond—sometimes it was better to let their actions speak for them. Sticking close to the wall of the tobacco stone, they forged ahead, and in no time at all they were up another level. The *obo* was roughly like a staircase; they simply had to keep climbing it.

"One…!"

"GBOOB?!"

One goblin who noticed the intruders below him found his throat slashed and died drowning in his own blood. Another who turned at the sound of his companion's death rattle was smashed by Lizard Priest's tail.

"GOOBGBBG?!?!"

"I believe they have noticed us!" Lizard Priest said.

"As if I care," Goblin Slayer replied. "It makes no difference to what I'll do."

They moved their pawns, as it were, up to the next level, working in perfect synchronicity. Dwarf Shaman's small frame could be seen gaining the newly secured level behind them. "I don't know about making the spell caster go first!" he groused.

"No choice. You're the slowest and clumsiest!" High Elf Archer said, and she was right. If they simply wanted to get to the top level, she would be the fastest. It would be difficult for an archer to secure fresh ground. Not that goblins were any match for a high elf, but it was a simple matter of their respective fortes. In every era and at all times, there has always been a place for the ax-wielding infantry soldier.

"C'mon, you too!" the elf called.

"Right…! Hup!"

Priestess clung to the rocks, working her way up behind Dwarf Shaman. Delicate, small, and—despite having bulked up a bit—not very well muscled, she was not very large or powerful. Still, she'd spent several years now adventuring like this, and she had started to get used to it. Her movements were hardly refined, but she ascended the rocks without difficulty.

"Oh..." And then she looked back. She should have realized.

"Hrk... Hrnn...!"

Behind her, Baturu was struggling along the rocks, trying to drag her equine body up the hill. Priestess saw it was the same problem they'd had with the wagon.

She didn't hesitate. "Here!" she said, holding out the bottom of her sounding staff.

Baturu looked from the staff to Priestess (who herself looked quite serious). Finally she said, "...Thank you... It's a help!" Then she grabbed the staff and heaved herself up the rocks.

Of course, Priestess alone couldn't support the centaur's weight. "A'right, there!" It was all the muscle packed into Dwarf Shaman's small body that made the difference. An uninformed observer probably wouldn't have known that it was muscle and not wine that had given his body the swells that it had.

"Hey, who knew dwarves could actually be useful?" High Elf Archer quipped.

"Less talking, more climbing!" Dwarf Shaman shouted at the guffawing elf.

High Elf Archer, for her part, hopped up the rocky hillside as easily as if she was bounding across flat river stones. Even as she went, she readied and loosed another shot.

"GOBBG! GOBBGB!!"

"GORGBGORRG!!"

Maybe these goblins hadn't noticed what was happening out front, or perhaps they thought these adventurers would make easier prey than the Dragontooth Warrior. Or perhaps the aroma of three young women simply drew the goblins like flies to honey.

Bein' an anvil's not enough to keep 'em away, Dwarf Shaman reflected as he grabbed the battle-ax at his hip and got ready to fight. "Don't worry about us down here, Beard-cutter!" he called.

Goblin Slayer, naturally, didn't reply. It was troublesome to have to worry about things other than himself. It was helpful to be able to let other people take care of them.

"GRG?!"

"Three…and four!" He met the goblin swinging a club from his left with his shield, bashing the creature to death; with his right hand, he swept out with his sword.

"GOOGBBG?!?!"

No need to strike a vital point in this situation. The goblin tumbled, his shin slashed, howling as he bounced down the steps. Even if he survived the fall, he wouldn't be crawling back up. Goblin Slayer begrudged even the time to glance back and see if the creature was dead. As he grasped the rock with his left hand and began to pull himself up, he thrust out with the sword in his right.

"GOBBB?!?!"

"Five!"

A goblin who had been trying to knock the stone free found his crotch savaged by the blade and collapsed, writhing. Goblin Slayer let go of his sword, giving the monster over to the fall. He had plenty more weapons.

"Six…!"

"GOB! GOBGRGB?!?!"

Goblin Slayer unhesitatingly picked up a rock and smashed it into a goblin's face. Crush the nose and it would pierce back into the brain. Even if it didn't go quite far enough, the creature certainly wouldn't be standing up again.

He cast aside the rock, which trailed threads of blood, and grabbed the goblin's club instead. Then once more without a moment's hesitation, he kicked the squirming goblin over the edge of the stairs.

"Hrah!" Lizard Priest's great form could be seen rushing across the stone steps he had secured, the claws on his hands and feet scoring the stone, limbs like logs holding him steady as he went. In the space of a blink, he was on the next level; it was a simple matter.

"GOBBGB!"

"GRGB! GGBOORGB!!"

Goblins rushed at him, one from the right side, one from the left, each crowing that they would do more than just watch him. Each of them thought the same thing: that the stupid one would die but the smart one (the thinker himself, naturally) would use that moment of opportunity to finish off the lizardman!

"Shaaaa!"

Do you suppose the goblins even had time to realize how naive they'd been?

One found his throat torn out; the other was slammed against the rock by a swipe from Lizard Priest's massive tail.

"GOBBGB...?!"

"Hmph!" Lizard Priest gave a great shake of his large head, then let the writhing goblin go. The creature tumbled through space, blood accompanying it as it came out of Lizard Priest's jaws. "One wishes one could wash the taste out of one's mouth!" he declared.

"There's cheese waiting for you when we get home!" High Elf Archer called. She had scrambled up on the rocks—or really, it looked as if the rocks had carried her up.

"Ah, now that is a reward worth fighting for!" Lizard Priest said, his tail wriggling.

High Elf Archer unleashed a hail of covering fire, up, down, and all around, opening a path for the two on the front row. Not to suggest that the three in the back were simply relaxing in the meantime.

"They're coming up from below!" The ax whistled. "And more of 'em every minute!" Dwarf Shaman cracked a goblin's skull open, then kicked him away, keeping the girls safe.

Priestess was trying to watch everywhere at once as she helped Baturu with the climb. Right, left, below—she left the area above to the others, but she wanted to know what was happening on the battlefield. Thankfully, the light of dawn had reached them here, the sun shedding its sacred rays on their position.

"At least they can't ride their wargs up here," Priestess said.

"Those things don't have enough limbs for it!" Baturu grinned. Was that a centaur joke?

Priestess smiled, too. She didn't quite understand, but whoever could smile during an adventure was winning.

Besides...

She was glad Baturu wasn't suffering too much as they focused on the climb.

Too often on adventures, she'd felt she wasn't able to be of any use.

But everyone had their strengths and weaknesses; that was just the way of the world. Priestess liked to think she understood that. And so…

"Watch out—they're coming from up top!"

…and so even when she heard High Elf Archer's shout, presaging the shadows that flew overhead, Priestess wasn't afraid.

"Goblin Slayer, sir," she said.

"Mrm…!" The man who had just smashed a goblin with a club responded by turning toward her.

The huge shadows that threatened to swallow up the adventurers came from an armful or two of large rocks. Maybe the goblins had dropped them, or maybe it was the work of that immortal sorcerer or whoever it was up there. It didn't really matter; the adventurers had to do something about it or they would "go to 14"—namely their deaths.

Even as he was still thinking, his arm was in motion, swinging mechanically, throwing the club.

"GBBOR?!?!"

A goblin who now had a club buried in his face fell backward, his arms and legs flailing. His death cry was drowned out by the rumbling of the stones, and Priestess didn't hear it. Instead, she heard a single sentence, nonchalant, almost mechanical: "I'll leave this to you."

"Right…!" She gripped her sounding staff and raised it high, focused her spirit, and raised her voice so that it might reach the gods in the heavens. *"O Earth Mother, abounding in mercy, by the power of the land grant safety to we who are weak!"*

The miracle was granted unto her. An invisible barrier that sprang from the very gracious heart of the Earth Mother herself soundlessly intercepted the stones. The deity had heard and granted the prayer of her pious young follower.

Diverted by the wall of light, the stones went flying in every direction. Goblins caught up in the chaos fell as they tried to escape or were crushed.

"Okay, let's go!" Priestess said with fresh resolve, holding out her staff to Baturu again.

"Right," Baturu said with a quick nod as she grabbed the staff and began scrambling up the rocks. "I must… *Ahem*, I have to say," she went on, picking her words, "that was…a most impressive display you put on."

"It wasn't me." Priestess puffed out her modest chest proudly. "It was all my friends—and the Earth Mother!"

§

"Blasted insects…!"

Was he referring to the adventurers or the goblins? Even the sorcerer wasn't sure. The chaos on and around the tobacco stone was already well beyond what he could allow. The goblins were jabbering ceaselessly, and the clanging of weapons was getting on his nerves. But what the immortal sorcerer found more unendurable than anything else was the centaur woman's stare, the way she just kept looking at him, completely silent.

"——"

It didn't matter that she was stuck on top of a mountain, with the burgeoning sunlight exposing her nakedness and humiliation for all to see. Still she stared straight through him with her clear eyes, as if he wasn't even there.

"What is it? Think you have something to say, girl?"

But the "girl" didn't answer. Even when the sorcerer walked over, grabbed her by the chin, and forced her to look up at him. She seemed as lifeless as a centaur-shaped doll—but he felt her warmth in his palm. The burning conflagration of a centaur's life force, far hotter than any human's. He found it deeply unpleasant, like touching grime or filth.

"Hmph!" He shoved her head aside like he was casting away a handful of mud. She fell prostrate, although her size and strength were far beyond his. Had she begun wasting away? Her skin seemed drained of blood, looking pale even under the dawn light.

A thought drifted through the sorcerer's mind—a memory of the tales of the white knights. Twelve knights with scales upheld had ended the summer of the dead. But it was the necromancer's pride that had proven the decisive move: Believing he was assured of victory, he had found the tables turned on him by the power of the scales at the last gasp. In a panic, he sought to borrow power from a demon, only to lose his soul.

What does she think, that I'm the same?

It wasn't possible. It wouldn't happen to him. Hadn't that necromancer, really, destroyed himself? This sorcerer was different. He wasn't like the others.

For if I was...

Then he would be just like those who had mocked and ridiculed him, and that was simply unimaginable.

The staff the sorcerer clutched in his hand creaked audibly. "...Never send goblins to do a man's job," he grumbled, sighing as he listened to the monsters howl and die. "I will go deal with this myself—and I'll do it quickly."

As he left, muttering to himself, the girl with the comet on her forehead watched him closely. Doing nothing. Saying nothing. As if he wasn't even there.

§

"There he is, above!" Lizard Priest called.

"Good," Goblin Slayer said with a nod as he kicked his sixteenth goblin off the rocks.

Compared with the "ladder mountain" and the Chief of Boulders that his master had forced him to free solo, this ascent was simple. Even he could do it, thankfully.

It's pleasing to know there's something even I can accomplish.

"Do you think he's noticed us?" Goblin Slayer asked.

"With the racket we've set up, I would be very much surprised if he hasn't," Lizard Priest said from the next rock up, climbing along with his tail curled.

"Fair enough." Goblin Slayer riffled through his item pouch for a stamina potion and pulled the stopper. "The problem is the goblins. And whether or not Silver Blaze is up there."

"I know that milord Goblin Slayer considers no time wasted if it is spent killing goblins!" Lizard Priest joked, and then, almost as an afterthought, he tossed a dagger down to Goblin Slayer. It was rusty and chipped but still very usable. "Goblin equipment—but perhaps worth your while?"

Goblin Slayer grabbed the dagger, checked the blade, and nodded. "It's a help," he said, stashing the weapon in his sheath. "It comes from this *obo*. Not bad."

One mouthful, two. He swigged a potion through the slats of his visor, seeking to restore his lost stamina. It was strange, how readily it helped the blood flow to his arms and legs. "The only other question is whether this Silver Blaze is in fact the centaur princess."

"Whoever Silver Blaze is, she's up there… Although so is that sorcerer everyone keeps talking about," High Elf Archer said, hopping up beside him like a leaf blown by the wind. Spotting an elf in a natural environment was famously difficult—even here on a pile of rocks. If nothing else, nobody doubted her abilities as a ranger. She grabbed another bud-tipped arrow from her quiver, her ears twitching. "No goblins up there with him. He's saying something, but I think he's just bellyaching. What do you think he's talking about?"

"I don't care."

"Aw, humor me." High Elf Archer grinned, but it was obvious she had no special interest, either. What she was focused on wasn't the sorcerer but someone else. As she checked her bowstring with the utmost seriousness, she said quietly, "We've gotta help the girl. That's what this adventure's about, right?"

"Adventure…" For a second, it sounded as if it was the first time Goblin Slayer had heard the word. "Yes, I suppose that's what this is."

"Sorry…to keep you waiting…," puffed Priestess, arriving belatedly on the rock shelf.

Baturu, holding on to Priestess's staff and assisted by Dwarf Shaman from behind, appeared after. The young centaur paid no heed to her own fatigue but said between gasping breaths, "Is the princess there?!"

"We don't know if it's your princess or not—but I think the woman called Silver Blaze is up there." High Elf Archer drew a line from her forehead to her nose with her pointer finger. "She's got chestnut hair except for a place right here that looks like a white falling star. She's very pretty—startlingly so."

"That's her! I'm sure of it!"

Baturu seemed about to fly to her princess, but Priestess held her back. It occurred to her to wonder whether what she was doing was rude to the centaur—not a very pertinent thought.

"You need to calm down," she said. "We have to think of a plan to rescue her first." She knew from her experiences hunting goblins just how dangerous a hostage could be. Baturu might be snorting and raring to go, but Priestess, standing beside her, tapped her lips with a thoughtful "hmm" and considered. "Maybe we could put them to sleep."

"Yeh understand that our opponent is a high-level spell caster, don'cha?" said Dwarf Shaman, who had finally gained the rock shelf with them. He took a theatrical swig of his wine and groaned. "We could try casting Stupor on him, but chances are he'd resist it."

"You used that spell on a dragon and you can't make it work on a little sorcerer?"

"Anvils can't talk, Long Ears!" Dwarf Shaman snapped.

The fact that he had no actual counterargument, though, meant he was admitting there was simply too much of a difference in strength. Anyway, before, they had been in a place of sand and earth, so the sand spirits had been particularly powerful.

High Elf Archer chuckled triumphantly. She looked up at the top of the hill, with the rocks to her back. "Well, assuming he doesn't have any arrow-deflection barriers, I can definitely hit him from here."

"...I've sometimes confronted sorcerers like that," came a quiet voice from inside the helmet.

"Ha!" the sharp-eared elf said, giving him a look and a nudge of her elbow. "You mean the quest you went on without mentioning it to us."

"There was no need to mention."

"It's common courtesy to let your friends know what you're up to!"

I see. There was a short nod, but that seemed to be all the more concern Goblin Slayer had for the subject. He began, "There are a number of possible moves. Gag him, blind him. Finish him off before he can intone a spell."

It was just like facing a goblin shaman.

"I see what you mean," Priestess said, nodding. In that case, it was clear what she had to do. "We'll go together, then."

"Guess I'll hang back," Dwarf Shaman said. Everything would not be decided with the first move. It was a sign of how serious this was that he even put the stopper back in his wine. "We might need Falling Control—if the anvil comes tumbling down."

"Careful, or *you* might need it," High Elf Archer shot back, glaring at him, but they had bigger things on their minds than a little argument right then.

That broke the tension. All that was left was the battle. An arrow sat loosely in High Elf Archer's bow.

Lizard Priest counted off on one clawed finger at a time, the gesture oddly somber: "Stifle the five senses, finish the foe in one fell swoop, rescue the princess." His reptilian eyes spun, taking in each member of the party in turn. "For these tasks, one wishes for a warrior who can close distances in a single bound."

"I'll do it," Baturu volunteered without hesitation. She got a firm grip on her katana, closed her eyes, and took a single deep breath. Letting her heightened emotions run all throughout her body, she repeated, "I will do it. To rescue the princess—that's why I came here."

"Then it's settled," Goblin Slayer said with a nod. He was still holding the empty bottle. "Let's go."

§

A whoosh of air signaled the start of the battle.

"Hrm!" The sorcerer turned, almost reflexively pointing his staff in the direction of the sound—but he saw no enemy. Instead, what came bouncing along the rocks was… "An empty bottle?"

"O Earth Mother, abounding in mercy, grant us peace to accept all things!"

Thus it took him a move, a moment, to realize what was really going on—a critical delay. For the moment the words of the prayer were intoned, all sound was stolen away.

Dog of the gods of Order! Accursed bitch!

The words of his curse, however, never took form. Instead, something pierced the sorcerer's right arm.

"Ngh…!"

He inhaled sharply; there was a shooting pain and a spasm of the physical muscles of his arm. As he tried to regain his grip on his staff, he discovered what appeared to be a branch growing from his arm.

No—it was an elven arrow. Where was the archer? No, no—there were more important things…

The way he opened his eyes wide, searching for the enemy, could not be called a miscalculation.

What entered his vision was an absolutely pathetic-looking adventurer. Cheap metal helmet, grimy leather armor. A small, round shield in his left hand. And in his right…

A stone?!

The sorcerer was about to bat away the projectile with his staff when suddenly there was a billow of thick black smoke. If there had been any sound in this space, one would certainly have heard the sorcerer's groaning shout. For the pain was intense and—so long as he had a flesh body with eyes and a nose—unavoidable. He flailed as if someone had stuck a sword in his eye.

Damn you…!

The sorcerer drew a figure in the air with the fingers of his left hand. There was a flash, a True Word—a word of true power—activating, rewriting the very logic of the four corners…

"Hooooaaarrrghhh!"

The scream rent the air, accompanied by the pounding of hoofbeats, originating from outside the silence. Or perhaps it was the shaking of the mountain that made him think there must be a noise—the centaur girl was running just that hard.

She poured everything into this moment, this second, this stroke of the blade. Her hooves split the rock beneath her feet, her legs like the wind. Her unsheathed blade as she raised it caught the ascending sun, glistening like gold. Though the sorcerer had never in his life felt such things were beautiful.

"…?!"

Therefore, as he uttered his voiceless cry, he felt only anger and resentment and hatred. When the sword sliced him in half, the blood splattered across the girl's beautiful face, defiling it. *Serves you right!* said the look on his face, to the bitter end, even as his body collapsed like a rag doll.

Baturu didn't spare the corpse even a glance but rushed forward. "Princess!" she cried, sound returning with another gust of the wind. Her voice was audible as she hurried forward.

Too much grander than she to be called a friend; too distant to be called an older sister. *Loyalty* was too cold a word, *love* too trivial. But when she called that precious name, there was an answering sound, an "ah" like the gentle noise of a lute being plucked.

The silver star shifted. The eyes were looking at the girl. Seeing her.

"Ah… You came. I see. Yes, you came… You came for me."

Silver Blaze gently embraced the girl who rushed to her, fell to her knees, and clung to her. How long must these recent days and months have seemed to Baturu?

"Gracious… So many tears. What am I going to do with you? I'm the one who's apparently being rescued." Pale fingers reached out, gently wiping the girl's eyes.

Baturu's head snapped up. She rubbed her red eyes and said, "I'm so glad you're safe. So, so glad…"

"Don't worry." Silver Blaze—or perhaps we should say the former princess of the centaurs—smiled shyly. "I was so focused on the next race that it didn't even bother me."

§

"I'm sorry. Could you lend me something to put over my shoulders?" Silver Blaze asked. It had grown quite chilly, and she was starting to shiver.

They were on the hilltop at dawn. It was probably the pouring sunlight and the high body temperature of a centaur that had allowed her to endure.

Baturu looked around, but the only thing she could find was the dead sorcerer's cloak. She could hardly make the princess wear *that.* She was just trying to decide what to do when—

oboru Kannatuki

"Um, you can wear this, if you don't mind!"

Priestess came trotting over, taking off her own cloak. She was flummoxed, though, uncertain where to put the garment, over the human part of the princess's naked body or the horse part. The pale, beautiful human flesh was the part Priestess found particularly distracting, but that wasn't to say that the princess's horse half wasn't beautiful. Neither was it something that should be exposed, to be viewed by all and sundry.

Moreover, a human like Priestess didn't know which part would help a centaur feel warmer. Finally, after much wondering, Priestess simply held the cloak out to the princess.

"H-here..."

"Thank you."

Silver Blaze took it and put it on with a smile so gentle, one would never have imagined she had been a prisoner until a moment before. Only then did she seem to register the people around her. She blinked, which emphasized her long eyelashes, and then she said, "*Ahem.* You must all be adventurers, yes? I'm very sorry for having put you to such trouble."

"That was the quest," Goblin Slayer told her. "It's no trouble."

"I suppose I should thank you, then...," Silver Blaze said softly. Her face suddenly took on a serious aspect. "Are we too late? Can we make the race? It's the biggest! I don't have a good sense of time in here."

"Princess, you mustn't overwork yourself...!"

"You can stop calling me princess," Silver Blaze said. She somehow managed to struggle to her feet, and Baturu hurried to support her. They didn't look like a master and servant, or like friends, or sisters, or even lovers. What existed between the two of them was nothing so simple or clearly defined as any of those.

But Priestess thought: *There's an intimacy between them.* That much was clear and, Priestess suspected, it was enough.

"She's...special, isn't she?" Priestess remarked.

"You think?" High Elf Archer said, her ears fluttering. "Isn't she just, like, how princesses are?"

An ambiguous smile was the only answer Priestess offered.

In any event, everything wasn't over yet. One might even say it was just beginning.

"What's the state of the goblins?" Priestess asked.

"One suspects they don't quite grasp the situation," Lizard Priest said, rolling his eyes merrily and sticking his head out to peek into the field. "They're still ravenous for battle. In fact, they seem to think they have us cornered."

"Yeah, and they're coming for us right quick. A whole slew of cannon fodder," Dwarf Shaman said, taking several drinks of fire wine to rev himself up. "We're smack in the middle of their net. How do you want to handle this, Beard-cutter?"

"This is actually ideal. We can take them all out in one fell swoop."

"Yes, you're right—you are so right."

The response came from none of the adventurers, who quickly brought their swords, claws, bows, and sounding staffs to the ready, facing the source of the voice—the tattered black cloak they had discarded. As they watched, a shadow seemed to stretch out from it, standing to phantasmal feet.

Goblin Slayer immediately swung his sword, but the shadow was faster.

"Survival is consumed by the sins of life, and life is consumed by the jaws of death."

"Hngh… Ah!" Baturu collapsed to her knees.

"Hey!" Silver Blaze said, instinctively calling out Baturu's name, holding her up.

"I'm…hngh…f-fine…" Baturu tried valiantly to stand, but her legs were weak and shaking. Her face was so pale that the blood spatter, which had grown dried and black, looked red again.

"Oh no…!" Priestess exclaimed. This was some kind of curse. She could see the muscles of Baturu's neck spasming.

"What just happened?!" High Elf Archer said.

At almost the same moment, Lizard Priest howled, "I see! So this is the Vital Drain spell!"

Vital Drain: a magical spell wielded by necromancers that enabled the caster to steal life energy from someone else. The ability had begun as a song in praise of life, ushering captive young lions into the future. But this was something else—someone on the edge of death stealing life from someone young and vital.

"That's unnatural! Inhuman!" Dwarf Shaman raged. "Is that the real secret to immortality?!"

"...The life of one who, in the course of a century, will accomplish nothing and be forgotten? How much more meaningful for that life to become a foundation stone in *my* immortality!"

The cloak no longer rested upon a shadow but upon a definite human form—the necromancer was regaining his identity as a sorcerer. He hardly looked like someone who'd been chopped in two mere moments before.

He disdainfully pulled the arrow out of his staff hand, breaking it in half and throwing it away. "You've upset my plans...but also brought me a gift. An even younger centaur and the life of a high elf besides!"

He opened the cloak with a flourish, and Priestess couldn't restrain a yelp of terror.

For there were faces.

People's faces. Humans, elves, dwarves, rheas, padfoots, even dark elves. They were young and old, men and women; the one thing they had in common was that they all squirmed and writhed across the sorcerer's torso. It was a sight that could have been created only by some devil, some demonic power far from any moral path.

Worse still, the faces appeared to be alive—or trapped in life. These people now existed only to feed the sorcerer's life. One could easily have gone mad when faced with such a truth.

Baturu, looking so pale that she could hardly stand up, leaned heavily against Silver Blaze. She was consumed by the realization that she would soon be one of those faces.

"I know not who you are or where you come from, but I thank you," the sorcerer said. "You are proof that even the scruffiest and most pathetic of us can do something worthwhile."

Goblin Slayer didn't say anything. He didn't have any interest in this. He didn't even think it was he himself who was being called *"scruffy"* or *"pathetic."*

He was simply digging in his pocket.

What do I have in my pocket?

He remembered the rhea cackling amid the blizzard in the icy cavern.

His own preparations. His party members—his party members' spells. This situation. The opponent's fighting strength. Suppose that— Yes. What had the sorcerer said?

"I know not who you are or where you come from."

That was it. And if this sorcerer, whoever he was, didn't recognize Goblin Slayer…

…Then he doesn't know how that *turned out, either.*

"So," Goblin Slayer murmured, "it appears it can be useful for your face to be well known."

He'd never particularly worried about it before, but it actually might have helped him at this moment.

He did some quick mental calculations, then asked, "Do you still have some left over?"

"Hrm? Ah, yeah," Dwarf Shaman said, briefly taken aback by the contextless question. He riffled through his bag of catalysts, and his eyes widened. The smile that came across his face then was like a child plotting some mischievous prank. "Yeah, I sure do."

The expression on Lizard Priest's face when he saw this was surely the lizardman equivalent of the mischievous child. "You have a plan, then?"

"Yes," Goblin Slayer said simply. "I always do."

INTERLUDE

Corner the Assassin!

My shoulders always get so damn stiff, the man thought as he exited the casino. He began rubbing aimlessly at his shoulder blades.

It wasn't the unsuitable clothing that got him—it was the ridiculous sword he had to carry around all the time. It was so heavy. If only he could have used a silver-painted wooden sword.

But the padfoots'd sniff that out in a second.

The smell of paint would be obvious to them, and his cover would be blown. So the sword was what you might call a necessary expense.

Other than that, that lot're stupid enough to make excellent product.

Thanks to that, he felt a warmth in his chest; the casino was a place of good memories for him. He was even grateful to it.

The alcoholic spirits coursing through his body left him pleasantly tired. He walked along, his feet feeling light and fluttery. It was nice. He took a swig from the bottle of alcohol he'd "borrowed" from the big, stupid, self-important padfoots.

The man had actually been an actor in another life. And also (if we want to be precise) a washed-out adventurer. It was the height of dumbassery, in his opinion, to put one's life on the line to earn some coin, the way you did when you were adventuring. Much better to make money *pretending* to be an adventurer. And if you were going to do that, then it was easier with some stupid padfoots than with anyone who knew what the hell they were looking at.

Eventually, he had realized that the padfoots—especially the centaurs—were far more valuable themselves than the admission fee they were paying.

It was a dark profession, one he'd had nothing to do with during his time as either a villager or an adventurer, but his connections from his days as an actor were proving very handy. Males and females both sold well—to men and women alike—and what was it to him if they were being carted off to be racers or to be taken to the pillow?

Not like they're being hunted for sport, after all. Well, maybe that was what some customers wanted to do with them—but if they did, so what? It was no concern of his. *Adventurers are all about taking responsibility for themselves, right?*

He went from tribe to tribe, telling tales of adventure with every bit of verve he could muster, pulling the wool over stupid young eyes and then carting off the fools. He would convince the ignorant kids to sign contracts that made them slaves, then sell them—that was his business now. A perfectly respectable trade, about which there could be no complaints. Or anyway, so the man believed.

His products typically couldn't read or write, but if he could get them to sign their name to a contract, they were his.

Speaking of which…

His purse was starting to feel a little light. He'd celebrated a bit too much over his recent successful business negotiation.

Well, so be it. He wasn't the saving type. If he earned it, he spent it; if he spent it, he had less of it; and when he didn't have enough, he earned again.

"Got to say, you don't see one as good as that very often…"

The kind of centaur you could be smitten with at first sight. A young woman who seemed to spend all her time in the field staring into the distance. She was so lovely that even this man, who had seen a fair few padfoots in his time, thought he might never see her like again.

Excellent bones, which meant excellent muscles. This centaur had been like a perfectly tuned musical instrument.

His first thought had been to sell her to one of the procurers, the people who sold young ladies to the brothels. Typically, the procurers sent centaurs on to houses of ill repute on the outskirts of town, places hardly better than stables—but this girl, she was different.

This is a chance to make some real money, the man had thought. He needed a place that dealt with the aristocracy. They would pay the girl's weight in gold to have her.

So why hadn't he done it? What had stopped him?

"I just love running!" That was what the girl had said, he remembered, as she went with him to the water town, all unaware of her fate. *"I don't mean running to fight or even to survive—just running."*

Well, all right. The man had decided to sell her instead to one of the *ludi* that trained racers. It didn't really matter to him, so long as he got a decent price. As for the girl, she could run herself to death for all he cared.

It had made his purse bulge, and the Four-Cornered World was none the poorer for it.

Now what do we do next?

The man wandered along with no particular place to go, looking for somewhere new to work, a din sounding distantly in his ears.

He thought about the minor commotion he seemed to have caused and considered the importance of not targeting too many centaurs in a row. Maybe a harefolk girl would be good next. Like the one who'd been hopping around the casino. He could sell her as a pretty little companion for someone. She'd had white fur…

Or wait, was it red? Were her ears pointy? Can't remember… He couldn't quite get his drunken mind to work. *Well, doesn't matter.*

"Boy, stupid adventurers are the best thing in the world!"

"Yeah, we oughtta be grateful!"

The man stopped in his tracks. He suddenly realized there was no one around. He was in some gloomy back alley. He didn't even know how he'd gotten here. He'd felt as if he was following a thread.

The voices came from behind him. He didn't recognize them. He took a deep breath in, then let it out.

"The Adventurers Guild dances to the government's tune, after all. You went too far."

No sooner had he heard the whisper than the man found himself flying to the right. There was a *thump.* A beat. Then something tore through his cloak—and his left arm, which lit up with a fiery pain.

"Gygax!" the man swore.

He was already reaching into the folds of his clothes with his other hand. It was a little trick he'd learned during his time as an adventurer—not a very impressive one, but...

...It's enough to save my life!

"Whaddaya want?! Money?!" he demanded.

"Wizball," replied the assassin—the runner. The man didn't know what it meant. His assailant was wearing a military-style cap that hid his face.

The man flung the dagger he'd pulled out without even looking at it, but it was batted away by some kind of small cylinder his attacker produced. By that point, however, the man was already running. He needed to get some distance. He turned the corner—anywhere, so long as he didn't go in a straight line.

"Hnnngh?!" he exclaimed as his ankle became entangled in a shadow. He tumbled forward unceremoniously, his eyes wide.

...That's not my *shadow!* he realized.

It looked like the jaws of some beast poking out from the darkness, clamped around his ankle. He tried to pull loose, but it was futile—you can't grab on to a shadow.

Then as he struggled, the man heard footsteps. He looked up to see the eyes of a bat shining in the night.

"Besmirching the name of good adventurers was going too far. They're like parents to us," a voice whispered lightly. It sounded younger than he'd expected. "This isn't like just counterfeiting a rank tag or something."

"Like hell!" the man yelped, glaring into the runner's bizarre eyes. "For your information, I haven't killed anybody! Me, I just—"

"Sold lives for profit. That's what it's called."

Give it up already. Those words took the form of the butt of the cylinder connecting with the man's head. The sound was heavy, dull, hard—more like a walnut cracking than his skull.

The sound signaled the end. The man gave one great twitch and went limp. The spy nudged his body into a corner of the alley with his foot, then let out a breath. "Sorry. Didn't expect his reactions to be so good."

"Hey, covering you is my job."

The voice definitely came from one or two corners past the alley. A red-haired elf appeared almost silently, except for a couple of clicks of her tongue. At the sound, the shadow rose from the dead man's—the coachman's—feet and came over to her in the shape of a wild animal. She patted it on the head and then allowed her own shadow to overlap with it, the two of them merging together.

"Besides, I don't want to leave the likes of him alive," she said, her voice cold and sharp enough to stab a person through. To the spy, it sounded like she was saying she wished she could have done the deed herself.

He knew her situation, more or less. He could guess. He was involved, sort of. That was exactly why…

"This is my position. Doing this stuff," he said evenly. Then he added, "Let's get back," and started walking.

The girl blinked in confusion before she said, "Yeah, right," and hurried after him.

They didn't talk.

Through the gloomy back alleys and shadows of the great city they went. There was a distant din. Footsteps of all kinds. The lights of the city didn't reach them.

Soon they would arrive at their carriage; their friends would be waiting for them. The spy pulled a cigarette from his pocket, and the girl took out a lighter without so much as a question. He leaned over, and she got up on her tiptoes a bit. There was a quiet *fwsh*, and some light illuminated.

"How'd it go again? *'There's no mastering a world upturned'*?"

"And you can't run away from your destiny."

The faint sweet smell of goji-berry smoke mingled with the scent of fire powder and drying blood, then wafted away. The red-haired girl looked in the eyes of the young man who was a spy. The bat-like light was gone.

He grinned, the edges of his mouth curling up, and said, "You do look pretty tempting…"

"Aw, stoppit!" The girl pulled her cloak over her uniform—but the rabbit ears still bobbed over her head.

CHAPTER 5

Leave It to an Adventurer!

"Fear not the chill of death, for you are only flesh, only a lump of meat!"

It was the immortal (well, so he called himself) sorcerer who took the initiative. His staff flashed with death-dealing lightning as he scattered the adventurers' formation. It was the most basic of basics when it came to responding to a Fireball, but it made it hard to cover each other. They couldn't be everywhere at once. Anyway, scattering was pointless in the face of a spell that hit the entire scene.

"What do we do about this?!" High Elf Archer asked, her ears twitching ever so slightly with the chill of death missing her by an inch. They'd already scrambled down the side of the hill anyway, so there were some obstacles between them and the sorcerer—but it was hardly safe ground. Her ears were sharp enough to pick up the sound of goblins working their way up the tobacco stone from below.

"GOROGGBB!"

"No one invited you!" she said, kicking away (with high-elven grace) a goblin that tried snatching at her ankle. The creature went bouncing down the hill, his body twisting and breaking as he went—but he was only the first. More and more goblins would reach the summit soon.

So High Elf Archer didn't begrudge her arrows, though she didn't have that many left, as she fired downhill. "We don't have a lot of time to play around with this guy!" she shouted. Whatever you called him. She cast a significant glance back up the hill, past the obstacles.

"What's the matter, adventurer? I think you lack something in ferocity!"

The basic problem wasn't the number of lives the sorcerer had—the faces squirming around as he gloated. No, it was the spell with which he had reached out toward Baturu.

No point in killing him if she dies, too! High Elf Archer thought.

They could try running, but there were no guarantees they would get away before the curse had its deadly effect. Neither did the elf believe, however, that this meant they were cornered, out of options.

Orcbolg had said he had a plan. He would certainly do something. Besides…

"We'll manage this…somehow!"

Her best friend, the one who'd been seriously poisoned by that weirdo, was there, too, calling out. Priestess could be seen supporting Silver Blaze, who was supporting Baturu, all of them among the shadows of more distant boulders.

"*Tonitrus…oriens…iacta!* Rise, thunder!"

She might yelp as the hideous miasma passed by her, but she wasn't afraid. She looked closely at Baturu, who was drawing small, quick breaths, her skin pale. Her face was splattered with blood, and her breathing was ragged. Even at that moment, it was clear, her life was being siphoned away.

"Will you…will you be able to help her?" Silver Blaze looked pleadingly at Priestess, squeezing the centaur's small hand. The look on her face was so sincere, so vulnerable, that the weight of it was almost painful. Priestess realized her throat was tight.

It would take such courage to say what she was about to say. It would have been wonderful if someone, anyone more capable than her was here in this place. But there was only her. She was the one they had.

So the only choice…is for me to do it!

"Please," she began, "leave it to an adventurer…!"

Priestess's voice rose as she went, until it became a shout, so that all the gods might hear her—so that *he* might hear her.

Then she looked firmly forward, her resolve set. "…I need some time!"

"All right," Goblin Slayer responded immediately from his place several obstacles up. "I'll leave the timing to you."

"Yes, sir!"

All he needed to do, then, was deal with the goblins. That made things very simple for him.

Goblin Slayer kicked a stone out from under his foot and observed it tumbling down. No, it wasn't exactly observation—more just making sure.

"GROGB?!?!"

"GOB?! GOBBGRBG?!?!"

The pebble smacked into other stones as it went, until the rockslide caught up several goblins. Effectiveness confirmed.

He had already seen that there were no spell casters among the oncoming goblins; if that sorcerer had any sense, he wouldn't want any other magic users serving him, least of all a goblin one.

If they could use magic, too, it would mean in the goblins' minds that they were just as good as he was.

As far as it went, that made this sorcerer a better commander of the goblins than that dark elf (he thought it was; he didn't remember) had been.

The goblins, scrambling along however they saw fit, were hardly powerful opponents, but they were the most dangerous thing there. If the party could deal with them, they could manage the rest somehow.

"Drop some stones on them, whatever you can find, to slow them down," Goblin Slayer ordered.

"Ah, physical labor! The province of dwarves and lizardmen!" Lizard Priest said.

"And here I thought we were supposed to be spell casters," answered Dwarf Shaman, but it didn't stop him from swinging his arms with a "here we go, then!" and knocking a boulder loose with his ax. A boulder that Lizard Priest then grabbed and flung…

"GOGBBGB?!?!"

"GRGG!! GOGB?!"

Goblins went tumbling everywhere, caught up by the stone, squashed flat by it, or else panicking even though they were in no particular danger from it. Those who were sharp-eyed enough to dive away from the oncoming boulder found themselves pierced by bud-tipped arrows that came flying from impossible directions.

It might not have accounted for too many goblins compared with the number encroaching upon them, but that was no problem, for it did indeed buy time—and time was what their party member Priestess had sought.

Meanwhile, the black-clad sorcerer watched the battling adventurers with leisure. "A little girl like you, undo a spell like mine? You're all talk!"

What was Priestess—fifteen? A little older? The words of such a small, young girl would never be enough to counter the sorcerer's pride.

Yet it's a sign of my magnanimity that I don't grow angry about it.

The cold touch of death once felt had cooled the passion of his thoughts and brought him a certain detachment. Even in the extraordinarily unlikely case that the girl did break his curse—well! That would be something to see!

He would regret if this little girl beloved of the Earth Mother should end up as nothing more than a walking womb for the goblins. Compared with the high elf, though, she could add only droplets to the ocean of his life.

The sorcerer chuckled. *If you can't break the curse, then you'll spend your last days entertaining my goblins.*

She might live for a night, two at most. Those who were of no use deserved no more.

"Very well. I'd like to see you try. I won't interfere with you," the sorcerer said. Instead, he pointed his staff at the scruffy man who had emerged from behind one of the rocks. Yes, a scruffy man indeed, much like those who were said to have lurked in that most infamous of dungeons.

The eyes under that helmet, however, were hardly looking at the sorcerer. He might as well have been a stone on the roadside.

Curse them all! the sorcerer thought. Everyone treated him that way, brushing him off like a silly child not worthy of their time. But now, now they would see. He was here, and he would grind them underfoot. Who was it who had placed their hand upon immortality? Not the wretched, ignorant masses but him!

"*Sagitta...inflammarae...raedius!* Fly, O fiery arrow!" The sorcerer let his emotions flow over into words of truth, the energy flying from his staff.

As he ran, Goblin Slayer pulled a stone from his pouch and flung it.

"How many times do you think your little tricks are going to work on me?" the sorcerer demanded.

He didn't think they were. But the tear gas would block the sorcerer's vision, and that would be enough.

Goblin Slayer's projectile met the bolt of flame in midair, the gas bomb bursting in a cloud of red powder. Lightning dropped where Goblin Slayer had been an instant before, shattering a boulder, and the resultant cloud of dust only helped him. He hid behind it as he reached with his free hand and grabbed one particular weapon—his newly refurbished, wickedly bent throwing knife. Goblin Slayer didn't exactly understand who this sorcerer was supposed to be, but it seemed like an opponent against whom he shouldn't hold back.

In any case, it's of a different value.

He threw underhanded, from the left, the knife describing a great arc as it flew.

"*Magna...nodos...facio!* Form, magical binding!"

The knife wasn't enough to cut through the mystical protection of Force Field.

But it's enough.

He'd forced his opponent to use up a spell. It was exactly what he'd expected, and the fact that the knife didn't get through to the foe was no fault of the weapon's. Goblin Slayer retrieved the throwing knife with the string he'd tied to it and started jogging again. He didn't imagine himself as professional enough to strike a quick, decisive blow, even if he'd first made the enemy flinch back with a strike from a spiked chain.

"Ha! So it turns out all you know how to do is run away with you tail between your legs!"

The sorcerer was yammering about something, but Goblin Slayer wasn't listening. There had never been any need to.

He's a goblin shaman who speaks human language.

That, in Goblin Slayer's mind, was all he was. And if so, then

Goblin Slayer could buy time against him just as well as against any goblin. And if he bought enough of it…

Then the more capable adventurers will be able to do something.

§

"Hoo… Hah…"

Priestess had likewise banished all extraneous thoughts from her mind. At that moment, for her, the four corners consisted entirely of the dawn light and her suffering friend.

Priestess's small chest heaved up and down as she sucked the dawn air into her lungs and then gradually let it out again. She took into herself the sacred force that saturated the world, cycling it through her, collecting it.

"Hh… Hngh…"

Priestess gently brushed Baturu's cheek, defiled as it was by dark blood, and closed her eyes. *I'm glad this isn't my first time,* she thought. Or was she? Perhaps that first time, she'd been better able to completely clear her mind. Now she felt a twinge of anxiety. She couldn't help wondering if she could do it. That didn't represent any lack of faith in the gods—but a lack of faith in herself.

But that makes it a failure of faith in the blessed Earth Mother.

A shadow of doubt that she would always hear the voice of her faithful.

No, no. I have to stop this.

It was no good to let her mind run in circles.

Random thoughts would never disappear completely. Instead, when she noticed them, each time, she had to get back to the original path. Protect, heal, save. She repeated those three in time with her breathing, then repeated them again. When she saw something else arise, she went back. Again and again, she repeated the process.

As she did so, suddenly, there came a moment when her mind was clear. The time when her soul was at its utmost.

It's all right.

The Earth Mother was a kind and gentle goddess. And *he* was fighting on her behalf.

And I am an adventurer.

Priestess prayed.

"O Earth Mother, abounding in mercy, please, by your revered hand, cleanse us of our corruption!"

No god would fail to answer the prayer of a Pray-er Character. None of the players in heaven would betray the Pray-er Characters down below. So long as the characters engaged in adventures, their "players" would be with them.

One could never be certain of success, but one could know that the dice of Fate and Chance would always roll. Thus, Priestess had made mistakes before, she had been forgiven, and her prayer had brought salvation. The all-merciful Earth Mother responded to her pious disciple by causing the Purify miracle.

"Oh... Ah..."

Baturu blinked several times at a pleasant damp feeling on her cheek. She brushed it with her fingers to discover it shimmering golden in the morning light.

It was water.

A clearer, purer water than she had ever seen in her life. The blood that had been suffused with the corruption of the evil curse no longer existed in this world. So naturally, the curse that had relied on that blood as a catalyst also disappeared.

I'm glad I got to her before the blood dried.

Then things might not have gone so well.

"This is incredible...," Baturu marveled.

"The Earth Mother truly is amazing," Priestess said, letting out a private sigh of relief. "Didn't I tell you?" She smiled.

With that, Priestess had used up her miracles. If she wanted anything else to happen, she would have to do it herself. Thus she modestly, but nonetheless triumphantly, puffed out her chest and shouted:

"Now!!"

§

"I can't believe it...," the sorcerer groaned at the strange sensation that suddenly assaulted his body. He didn't know what the little girl had done, but was it possible she had actually broken his curse?

No, it couldn't happen. Such a thing was impossible, or so he believed. For if he had imagined otherwise, the prideful thought that followed could never have arisen in his mind.

But do I care? Ha!

He thought of all the many lives he had buried within himself by the demon's power. And how many lives did *she* have? One. Just one. He could capture that life.

"...!"

He took a breath—but before he could begin chanting anything, Goblin Slayer was moving. His right hand flashed, and a sword he had pulled from the *obo* sliced through the air.

It came from he knew not where; he had taken it from the hand of a goblin, but it was a weapon just the same. If the spell caster's concentration had been broken and the protection of his magic had vanished, then it would be perfectly able to do its job.

"Gah?!"

The decaying, rusty blade lodged itself in the sorcerer's chest, and he pitched backward dramatically. He did not die, of course. This wasn't one of the blades forged by that ancient people to bury the black riders. Just because it stabbed him, it hardly dispelled the magic holding him together. Even as the flame of his life guttered and he hacked up bloody vomit, he rose once more to his feet.

However...

"Fairies, fairies, never tarry—what you forgot, I give back fairly! I don't need cash, but make me merry!"

Dwarf Shaman wasn't about to let him get away with it. He flung his jar on the ground again, and the endless oil began flowing forth. The scented oil the fairies had forgotten, which was so valuable precisely because it meant nothing in terms of real-world worth, flowed like a sea over the hilltop.

"Hrn... Hgh! Grrr!"

Slip, slide, tumble—the sorcerer let out a humiliated shout as he floundered in the waves of oil.

"How could a mere child's prank...?!"

He tried to pull the sword out of his chest, but his hands slipped off it. His body slid so that he couldn't stand up. It was all he could do to clutch his staff to himself so that he might not drop it.

But so what? What is any of this to me?

He could not lose his life. A little oil, a little tumbling, so what? Did they think—?

"O proud and strange brontosaurus, grant me the strength of ten thousand!"

The sorcerer's upturned eyes were met with the sight of a terrifying naga, a lizardman dashing toward him, making the utmost of the strength he had borrowed from his forebears.

"Eeeeyaaahhh!" the lizardman cried, the claws of his feet punching through the film of oil to tear at the rock, carrying him forward without so much as a quiver.

When the sorcerer realized that this monster was making a beeline straight for him, he shouted something. Maybe it was a spell. Maybe a curse. Maybe a simple imprecation. Or maybe it had no meaning at all.

Whatever it was, the adventurers never heard it, for in the next instant, a tail, brought to bear with the lizard's full strength and speed, vaporized the sorcerer's jaw and sent him hurtling through the air.

"...?!?!?!"

Then the waves of oil carried him down the tobacco stone, bouncing him off every rock along the way. He couldn't even cry out, and any attempt at resistance would be futile. If he could have gotten the sword out and jammed it into a rock, he might have been able to arrest his fall, but the oil covering him from head to foot wouldn't let him.

Each time he smacked a stone, he felt a bone break or an internal organ burst, chipping away at his body.

The time until he finally struck the ground of the Four-Cornered World did indeed feel like an eternity.

§

"Hmm! I daresay he's still alive."

"He is unexpectedly tenacious."

Lizard Priest and Goblin Slayer were looking down at where the sorcerer had become a dark stain on the ground. With virtually every bone and muscle in his body shattered, even someone with immortality would have trouble rising again.

That ogre (is that what he was?) claimed to be immortal, too, but this is something different.

Goblin Slayer grunted quietly. There were indeed so many things he didn't know in this world.

"Well, we never did undo his actual immortality," Dwarf Shaman said as he flicked a coin through the air. "What did yeh expect?" The coin turned filthy the instant it dropped into the ocean of oil. The oil promptly vanished—almost like magic—leaving only the otherwise useless gold piece. "I think I should point out that we haven't actually finished this one yet," the dwarf added.

That much was true.

"GROGB! GBBOGBRG!!"

"GOGGBRGBBGR!!"

Now that nobody was dropping stones on them anymore, the goblins' advance resumed unhindered. Sure, arrows occasionally took one of them out, but everybody else just assumed the victims were the especially stupid ones.

"Blast it all! How does it end up being goblins *again*?!" High Elf Archer howled, meanwhile firing off three arrows in the blink of an eye.

One couldn't help but agree with her. The goblins looked like ants swarming a sweet treat on the ground. Then there was the sorcerer, who continued to squirm despite having been smashed against the earth.

Time was not the adventurers' friend. Every moment, the end was coming nearer. Death grew closer even as they stood and thought.

But that means nothing.

It was just another way of saying they were still alive.

Priestess, who stood flanking Baturu with Silver Blaze, nodded. If they were still alive, then all they had to do was do everything they could do for as long as they could do it.

The sun had now shown itself fully over the edge of the board, shining upon all the four corners.

They were on an *obo*. They were surrounded by a goblin horde. Rocks. The attack earlier. Using the terrain.

What would Goblin Slayer do? Priestess wondered.

Ah! Yes. She knew.

"Let's break this place apart!"

Without hesitation, Goblin Slayer said, "My thoughts exactly."

§

High Elf Archer looked up at the heavens—although it didn't do much good, as the Earth Mother was hiding her face. "Arrrgh… How does this happen?"

"Oh, um, of course I understand that this is a very important and most precious *obo* mound," Priestess said quickly. "But this holy ground has been defiled, and I can't purify it by myself…"

Not to mention that even if she could have, she had used up all her miracles. As a cleric, she simply didn't yet have what it took. Perhaps Sword Maiden, one of the famous All Stars, would have been a different story, but it just wasn't possible to ask her to come all the way out here to do a purification at this moment in time.

"But, uh, having said that, I hadn't quite figured out how to actually bring it down…"

"Let me handle that." Goblin Slayer did not hesitate. In fact, it looked like he probably already had something in mind.

The whole party knew full well what this man was likely to do.

"But do you suppose it would be…not such a good thing to destroy this mound?" Lizard Priest ventured.

"It's true that a lot of us don't know much about the centaur faith," Dwarf Shaman said, not begrudging to wet his tongue with the last of his wine. This was when the real fun would begin: When they fell, it should be with no strength left, not even any wine. "Maybe we should ask our fair ladies."

"Personally, I'd feel better rebuilding it from scratch." Silver Blaze's expression was too ambiguous to call a sad smile but too clear to imagine she wasn't thinking about the matter. Then she brushed a hand gently through the hair of the young centaur leaning against her side. "However..."

"Princess?" The girl who had only moments before regained her pallor looked at Silver Blaze in surprise.

"I've left this place behind. It's you, who still lives out in the fields, who should decide."

"........."

For a very, very long moment, Baturu didn't answer. She bit her lip, her expression hard, and looked, not quite at the earth and not quite at the sky.

They could hear the jabbering of the encroaching goblins. Smell the faint remaining whiff of blood. And feel the wind that pressed all of it upon them.

The wind. The wind was blowing.

There beneath the dawn sky, the wind ran to the very farthest edges of the plain.

Ahhh...

She saw now that the princess had no intention of coming home. That, to her, felt like an answer. It told her what she should choose.

"...Do it. Please. Bring it down."

Her verdict was just that brief. Baturu was looking straight at Priestess—and Goblin Slayer. At the cheap helmet with the broken horns. She still didn't know what expression the face beneath wore.

No, she didn't know, but she knew the man accepted her and her request.

What made her think that?

"All right," the helmet said, nodding up and down without missing a beat. "I will."

Quickly, calmly, almost mechanically, he began to spell out for them the plan he'd concocted in his head. High Elf Archer's ears drooped farther and farther as he spoke, while Priestess nodded and said, "I see."

As for Silver Blaze and Baturu, they didn't quite seem to understand the situation yet...

"Myself, I can still use a miracle. If you wish," said the warrior monk of the lizardmen, his tail curling with eager anticipation of battle.

If he was that excited to fight, Dwarf Shaman could hardly not come up with some mischief of his own. "Guess I'd better step up, too. No real point knockin' this thing down if we take ourselves with it."

The saying goes that three heads together are as good as the God of Knowledge, but *these* three heads were like naughty children planning a prank.

They do say that three naughty brats together can even chase away a grim reaper, High Elf Archer reflected. "It's because *you* two never stopped him that this poor girl wound up contaminated by Orcbolg."

"I d-don't think I'm contaminated…!" Priestess protested, struggling weakly against the sympathetic hug High Elf Archer gave her.

The five of them might have been standing in the middle of a battle zone, but they practically looked like they were enjoying themselves. Maybe that was part of what it meant to be an adventurer. Or maybe that was what it meant that this was an adventure.

Baturu could only blink.

I see now…

This was indeed something one didn't find on the plain.

§

"Are you sure this is…even possible?!" Baturu almost shouted. She was holding a rope wrapped around one of the boulders at the top of the hill.

Ah, rope: Never leave home without it! The grappling hook was secured firmly to the rock, while the party members held the other end.

"If you can win by doing the impossible or the ridiculous, then it's no trouble at all…," Priestess said, as if it was the most natural thing in the world, while she tugged on the knot to make sure it was firm.

High Elf Archer jabbed Goblin Slayer in the side with her elbow.

"Hrm," he grunted.

"Couldn't you teach her anything more *helpful*?" she said. Then she added grudgingly, "Granted, it's a little late now."

Goblin Slayer grunted again. "That is helpful, isn't it?"

"Yeah, I guess so." High Elf Archer knew that. She sighed in resignation, then chuckled (not without a note of fondness) and grabbed the rope. "Why not say something to her, too, then?"

There were Lizard Priest and Dwarf Shaman, prepared to the utmost. Across from them stood Silver Blaze, with Baturu beside her, looking anxious. The strangest thing was that Silver Blaze, the former prisoner, appeared to be the most vigorous of them all.

Goblin Slayer spent a moment in thought, then said, "I've heard deer can do this. Would it be difficult for centaurs?"

"...We'll do this, all right!" Baturu exclaimed, freshly invigorated, practically baring her teeth. The message was clear: *Don't mock me.*

Naturally, he hadn't had the slightest malice in mind; he had meant only and exactly what he said. Still, no one could expect a centaur to stand by quietly when their kind was compared with deerfolk.

For her part, Silver Blaze laughed—"Ha-ha-ha!"—as if she was genuinely enjoying herself and held tight to the rope. "We'll have to run as fast as we can, then."

"Huh? Wait! Princess...?!"

"I haven't run in *days*! I need to get practicing again!" She sounded like a child excited about her first game, and it brought a breath of relief from Priestess.

The rope was secure. The party was all together. And the other two...

They look like they're going to be just fine.

Once she had double-checked everything, Priestess turned to Goblin Slayer and nodded.

"All right." Goblin Slayer grasped the rope where it was secured at his own hip and braced his feet. "Anytime!"

At that, Dwarf Shaman scrambled up onto the boulder with his stubby arms and legs. He might have wished for a rock big enough for all of them to ride on, but you couldn't have everything. Even if Lizard Priest had managed to fit his great bulk atop the stone, getting two centaurs up there would have been awfully tricky.

Gotta work with what yeh have, Dwarf Shaman thought. Then he slapped his palm down on the great rock and drank the very last drops of wine from his jug. "Ready to roll, Scaly!"

There at the figurative tail of the party, secured to the rope just like the rest of them, was Lizard Priest, who howled: *"O my forbears who sleep under layers of rock, with all the time that has piled upon you, guide this object!"*

The sound was like a landslide. Touched by Lizard Priest's prayer, the great boulder that lay at the base of all these stones that had been piled up over countless ages buckled and crumbled under the vast weight of time. The *obo* became like a huge pile of pudding collapsing under its own weight. The rocks that made the tobacco stone, built up over so long, scattered in every direction, raising a cloud of dust. One stone smacked into another, cracking it, smashing it, sending it rolling away in some other direction.

To someone watching from a distance, it probably wouldn't have looked that fast—but that was an illusion created by the size of the stones. If you were right there in the middle of it, you knew exactly how fast it was happening.

The hail of stones was like a storm; they were like great war hammers and terrible blades. If you were sucked into the maelstrom, you would be torn apart, battered to pieces; your life would be forfeit. And it was all happening much too fast to run away from…

"Come out, you gnomes, and let it go! Here it comes, look out below! Turn those buckets upside-down—empty all upon the ground!"

However, the adventurers, and the great boulder they were tied to, flew at an impossible speed. Yes, flew. It didn't roll but shot straight downward, sliding along.

"Eep! Yikes, yikes, yikes!"

Priestess suddenly found herself kicking her legs, trying to hurry along with the rock. Of course, the footing was falling out from under her as she went; it was like pushing off the hillside and jumping. For indeed: The adventurers tied to the boulder were, like the boulder itself, under the influence of Dwarf Shaman's Falling Control spell.

Priestess clung to her cap lest it fly away, focusing only on not tumbling.

This is a lot like…!

When they had skied down the snowy mountain or when they had ridden on the back of the sand manta.

Are we going to die here?!

This felt dangerous enough to bring the thought to her mind—which made it all the more striking when she heard the giggling of the unseen faeries.

Ah, but…I'm not so afraid.

Not so afraid as she had been when faced with the red dragon, or in the water town sewers, or on that very first adventure…

The thought somehow brought a smile to her face. Even if it was a smile strained with a certain amount of terror.

"Is…everyone…okay?!"

"Orcbolg…has to be the biggest idiot…!" High Elf Archer shouted back, which Priestess took to mean she was all right. Even with the tips of her long ears pressed firmly back against her head, the high elf still managed to look elegant as she slid along. Priestess couldn't even picture her tumbling unceremoniously down the hill.

"Agh! Yipes! Argh!"

In contrast, the look on Baturu's face could be summed up in one word: *desperation*. She was gritting her teeth—she was hardly used to climbing rocks, let alone sliding down them.

Then again, none of them was exactly used to this. How could they be? All the same, Baturu kept running—if she stopped, she would die. Anyhow, she had her friend, Silver Blaze, beside her. Baturu saw Priestess look at them, but she didn't have the wherewithal to shout back. She settled for meeting the cleric's eyes and nodding. That was enough for Priestess.

"Goblins…ahead!" Silver Blaze shouted at that moment. She saw the green shadows lurking along the path of the rolling stone. "Still plenty of them…!"

"It won't be a problem!" Goblin Slayer called back.

The first enemy they made contact with was a goblin who had just happened to avoid slipping away in the earlier fighting. He had slid a short distance but—happily or unhappily—had managed to stop himself with his weapon. That, however, did not change the fate that awaited him.

"Hmph!"

"GROORGB?!?!"

As Goblin Slayer came hurtling down along with the boulder, he literally kicked the creature to his doom.

"GBBGR?! GBGBGRRROGB?!?!"

The monster slid down on a diagonal, breaking his bones, tearing his flesh, and shortly dying.

Nor was that goblin the unluckiest of them.

"GBBO?!"

"GOBOOB?!?! GBOGOBOGOB?!?!"

Several of the others became fodder for the hail of falling stones. Their death rattles didn't even reach Goblin Slayer's ears, for the great, ceaseless rumble drowned out their cries, the sounds of their flesh ripping and their bones shattering.

"Keep us going, dead ahead!" Goblin Slayer shouted. There went another one. It had tried to grab onto the rock in hopes of escaping. "If the rocks fall on us the moment we reach the bottom, this will all have been for nothing!" Gravel went pinging off the metal helmet. Elf or centaur ears could presumably pick up the individual clinks as the stones went flying around.

Priestess, likewise, felt rocks stinging her through her cap. She didn't have the courage to look up.

"Just keep a close eye on how our rope's doing!" Dwarf Shaman bellowed. "If it snaps, we're done for!"

"Right…!" Priestess didn't know whether he could hear her—she could barely hear herself or anyone else. They were all pushing as hard as they could. Trampling goblins, running along, thinking only of survival.

Priestess thought of her party members. She thought of them all going home together. She thought of her friends.

All those thoughts filled her head, so that she completely forgot about the sorcerer.

§

"Gah… Ah!"

Speaking of the sorcerer: True to his claimed immortality, he was still going despite his entire body having been crushed. He lay there on the earth where he had been flattened, trying desperately to get his limbs in a functional state, suffering. If someone were to be crushed by a giant, then hung by their neck, they might begin to grasp the intensity of his pain.

Damn...those...adventurers!

Ignorant, worthless bastards, utterly beneath comparison with him. Yet the likes of them had managed to interfere with his great self, had been able to trip him up. That was not to be countenanced. He *would* have his revenge.

He needed to repair his flesh and knit his bones as quickly as possible and get going again—he begrudged every minute, every second. When he had himself back together, those barbarians would be as nothing before him.

Even at this point, the sorcerer had learned nothing, saw no lessons in what he had experienced. Just as he had always blamed others for all the ridicule he had endured. He was, in one sense, perhaps not wrong to do so. Many are those who will point and laugh at someone simply for harboring grand ambitions.

But the sorcerer had completely forgotten about all the things he himself had done. He had no recollection of how many people's hopes and dreams he had trampled upon to get where he was. He wasn't even aware of them. He had simply assumed all was his right. It was pride—and it was his blind spot.

And then pride took the form of an immense, numbing weight and a cascade of gravel.

"Oh—ahh... Ahhh...?!?!"

The sorcerer didn't understand what had happened. He felt only a tremendous weight fall upon him, smashing the flesh and bones he had worked to repair. He had tried so hard to use the last glimmers of life in him to come back from the brink, only to be rebuffed by the stones.

The sorcerer found himself unable to move a finger, unable to draw a breath.

Why had it never occurred to him that to be immortal didn't mean to be invincible, and immortality was not eternity?

Why had he been satisfied to make immortality his goal? Yes, there were ancient things in the Four-Cornered World, like the kings of the dead, who had braved death to live forever. Perhaps, had he sought something more, the sorcerer would have had an opportunity to aim even higher.

But any opportunity for thought was snuffed out when a boulder landed on his head, crushing it and scattering his brains to the four corners, leaving behind only a lump of flesh that no longer knew what it was.

§

Almost before she knew what was happening, Priestess found herself standing in a billowing cloud of dust. Her feet were on solid ground. Her body was in one piece. The goblins were gone.

What about the others…?

"I don't know if he was immortal or what, but if you bury him, he won't be back."

Ah, there they are.

Priestess breathed a sigh of relief to see the man standing calmly there. Goblin Slayer was safe. Covered in dust and dirt, yes—but he was always grimy anyway.

Everyone else was there, too.

"Because he's unlike a goblin," Goblin Slayer added. The sorcerer, he averred, was far easier to deal with.

Priestess assumed Goblin Slayer was already thinking about the goblins who had been crushed or perhaps how to take care of the ones who had gotten away with their wargs. Dwarf Shaman, sitting on top of the boulder and bemoaning the fact that his wine was all gone, growled, "Give it a century or two and he'll come crawling back out, I suspect."

"It won't matter to me then."

"Yeah, but it might matter to *me*," High Elf Archer said, leaning back against the boulder and looking at the remains of the *obo* with a sigh. Then she shrugged, smiling as if to say, *These things happen.* "I can't believe we set out to rescue a centaur princess…and ended up fighting goblins!" *I predicted as much!* She groaned loudly, followed by another sigh.

"…You'd rather have been attacked by a dragon?" Silver Blaze asked seriously.

"I think I've had my fill of dragons, too." High Elf Archer laughed.

I think I get it now, Priestess thought. Princesses were like that: free, headstrong, like the wind. She shared a glance with Baturu. Priestess thought she understood now what it was between the warrior and Silver Blaze. Something much like what bound herself and High Elf Archer.

"...We'll just have to start piling the rocks again," Baturu said and smiled. A smile like the blowing wind, with none of the tension that had filled her face until that moment. A natural smile that showed that she could accept what the future held. "Plenty of centaurs and other travelers pass this way. I'm sure the *obo* will rise again in time."

"Do you think we should set up a stele or something?" Priestess asked jokingly and giggled. "You know, something that says, *Beware, for here an evil sorcerer lies sealed*."

"And then, a hundred years from now, the unwary, believing the warning to be mere superstition, will dig him up, and he'll come back to life." Lizard Priest bared his fangs merrily, though there was nothing merry about what he was saying.

He cheerfully began undoing the rope. "I'll help," High Elf Archer said, going over to him. Her delicate fingers were far more suited to this work than the long, sharp claws of a lizardman. "Humans do act like that, don't they?" she said.

"And so the seeds of adventure never run out in the Four-Cornered World," Dwarf Shaman added. What could a human like Priestess do but smile ruefully?

"It's not worth worrying about," Goblin Slayer said very softly—like a wish, like a prayer. Let it be a century; let it be two. Let it be a millennium. Whenever it happened, if it happened, then when that time came...

"Just leave it to an adventurer."

§

The cheers at the water town arena brought the house down. The prize that day was a grand one, named after a baroness who had been paraded naked through the city, once upon a time, to punish her for imposing crushing taxes. The contest took her name because, according to one story, she had been a centaur herself.

"Not that that's particularly credible," Female Merchant said with a twinkle in her eye. "But this is a festival, not a history book—and it's a good excuse to make merry."

They were in the stands of the racecourse, in the very best seats, where the nobles sat. The stand was shaded by a roof; you could see the entire course at once, and there were soft pillows to sit on—very much a place to relax and watch a race. Naturally, only Female Merchant's most cherished friends were invited there.

Today, for the occasion, she offered them sweet treats prepared with cacao, the so-called "bean of the gods."

"And to top it all off," she said, "today is—"

"The day Silver Blaze makes her grand return!" High Elf Archer finished, adding a "thank you" as she grabbed one of the brown sweets and popped it in her mouth. She immediately discovered a sweetness that ran from her tongue straight up to the tips of her ears, accompanied by a faint undercurrent of bitterness. It was like no fruit she'd ever tasted in the forest. Sugar truly was something magical—perhaps even fiendish.

Shivering, the high elf let out a sigh. "Incredible...!"

"Hrm," remarked Baturu, picking up one of the treats herself. "This little thing, you mean?"

"I meant that princess of yours," High Elf Archer said. "But the candy, too."

Still looking somewhat dubious, Baturu put the candy in her mouth—whereupon her ears stood straight up, the sweetness assailing her as it had High Elf Archer. The shock seemed to travel all the way to the tip of her tail before subsiding a few seconds later.

Baturu let out a breath like she might melt—and then she gazed into the distance. "Yes. The princess...is indeed incredible."

She had cast her eyes down over the huge crowd that filled every seat in the spectator stands. Then she looked at the centaur racers, pelting along the track with utmost commitment.

The earsplitting shouting. The young women dashing like the wind, moving as fast as they could.

There would be winners, and there would be losers. It was a serious competition—that was necessary. But all the racers would be feted by the crowd, would be given their due.

Only the princess, however, the one they called Silver Blaze, could attract a crowd quite this size. Baturu felt sure that if she had tried her entire life, she could not have done the same.

"So what are you going to do after this?"

The unexpected question from High Elf Archer pulled Baturu out of her reverie. "A good question," she said, but the answer had been settled long ago. "I suppose I'll go back to the open plain. I need to report to my older sister, you see. Although she seems likely not to be very happy," Baturu added with a wry smile.

High Elf Archer agreed wholeheartedly. "Older sisters never are!"

"Yes. One is grateful for them, but they can be a real headache!"

The two nodded at each other, shared a look, and then giggled like little girls.

That's right, Female Merchant recalled belatedly. The elf was the younger sister of something like the empress of the elves. She hadn't exactly forgotten that fact, but she'd simply been far more conscious of her as a friend. And too—if only once or twice and only on rather strange adventures…

A traveling companion.

Yes, perhaps she might be allowed to call her that as well.

Female Merchant put a hand to her chest, making her relief plain to cover for her embarrassment. "Everything has ended well. That's what's most important to me," she said. And it was entirely true. Certainly, it was important for those involved in the entertainment business. There were no guarantees their own centaurs might not have gotten caught up in things. And if it had turned out to be a matter of match fixing or some kind of cheating ring…

Well, I'm just very glad it wasn't.

Anything that put the pinch on entertainment would affect profits. And dwindling profits would lower the value of the racing centaurs. People would be less excited to watch them race. From olden times, there have been those who felt that the inability to generate profits demonstrated that one was of no worth. Female Merchant understood that painfully well.

She'd heard that the detective who'd allegedly been brought in was satisfied with the outcome as well. When he'd learned about what had happened, he'd supposedly said something about justice being served.

If that sorcerer really was sealed away...

And with the servant who had killed the lanista apprehended, all was well that ended well.

"I guess that wraps everything up," Female Merchant said as if to reassure herself, and she smiled.

Fwwwooo. The heat of the packed arena was leavened by a pleasant breeze that came flowing through. The lovely wind only stirred up the people's excitement and joy even further.

"This town, these competitions, adventures... In the end, they don't make much sense to me," Baturu said quietly. "I don't know what you're so excited about, and I don't know why my older sister and the princess left our homeland." But although she didn't fully understand... "I do see there's something here that we don't have on the plain."

"Yes," Female Merchant agreed.

"Yeah... I think you're right." High Elf Archer nodded.

They had tried their hands at adventuring because they'd wanted to find something that was lacking in their noble house or their forest home. They had lost some things and gained others. Things they would most assuredly never have gained had they simply stayed home.

But not everyone sought to pursue such things in their lives. For Baturu, this adventure was a strange and unusual occurrence. She was certainly not an adventurer, not someone who made her living adventuring.

"But," Baturu said, "I have found some things we share."

"Such as?"

"The wind." Baturu looked at her friend, then past her friend, beyond the spectator seats, where she could see the great spreading sky. A gust caressed her cheek, playing with her hair, dancing as it went by. "The wind blows here, as it does in my home. So all is good."

Baturu smiled, the same relaxed smile she'd given them at the tobacco stone, open to the future. "Therefore, I will go back. And it's not as if my older sister or the princess will never come home so long as they live, is it?"

And when they returned, Baturu would be there to welcome them on that open field with its heartening breeze.

The sky was the same sky in all the four corners; the wind was the same wind. And if there were things you couldn't find at home—well, there were things you could find only at home, too.

"Everyone's got their own path to walk," said Dwarf Shaman, who had been listening silently until that moment, more focused on the race and his wine. He tucked a betting ticket into the folds of his robes, looking pleased about it in a way that suggested he'd picked a winner. Then he grinned, showing his white teeth. "So long as yeh stay on that path, you can walk with your head held high."

Right.

It was Female Merchant who nodded at Dwarf Shaman's words. She didn't believe the path she had once walked was mistaken. She may have fallen and been hurt—but she was pulled to her feet and got up, and it had led her here. It was why she had this moment—and with this moment she was supremely satisfied.

"Hmm?" High Elf Archer said, glancing at Lizard Priest. "You haven't tried it yet?" Her attention had already wandered from the conversation, fixing on the treats Female Merchant had brought.

"Our people use this as a stimulant..."

"It's got cow's milk in it, so it's pretty much like cheese, isn't it?"

"It has its similarities but also its differences—mm, but nectar this is. Nectar!"

Apparently he liked it.

Even with a massive lizardman sitting beside a centaur, there was plenty of space in the noble seating. High Elf Archer glanced around with much interest. She saw that even the weird-looking adventurer in their midst caused no real consternation.

"Sorry to keep you waiting," he said as he arrived.

It was totally understandable if the people in these prime seats did a bit of a double take. In fact, they probably deserved an award for managing to keep it to a modest flinch of their expressions, given that someone who looked like Living Armor was working his way past them. Female Merchant was unable to suppress a bit of a smile as she offered an *it's okay* gesture in their general direction.

"You're late, Orcbolg!" High Elf Archer said.

"It hasn't started yet, has it?"

"Well, no," she admitted, but she puffed out her cheeks indignantly nonetheless.

Goblin Slayer took that for the end of the conversation and strode to a random seat.

"How'd it go?" Female Merchant asked, offering him a cup and politely pouring some wine for him. "Did she say you could have it?"

"When the race has been run, I'm told," he said, his usual brief response. *"It"* was nothing special in and of itself—but they were dealing with Silver Blaze here.

There must be many who want it.

But if there was anyone here who could get it, surely it would be none other than these adventurers.

"I've heard something about it being a good luck charm... I don't really understand." He took a swig of wine as if it were water.

Where were his eyes looking behind that metal helmet? He seemed to be gazing off into the spectator seating, watching the crowd cheer themselves silly at the centaurs, as if hailing great heroes. He was watching them wait expectantly for Silver Blaze.

Finally, he grunted softly, nodded, and said, "I do understand that your princess is quite amazing."

"Yeah." Baturu also nodded. "I absolutely agree!"

Her princess was amazing. She spoke the words with utmost pride.

Then there was a tremendous cheer. Another race was finished, another winner made. The victor would be crowned with glory, while the losers would be congratulated on their fine effort, for there was none there, not one, who had failed to give their utmost.

"You're alone?" Female Merchant asked, tucking her head. "What about the girl?"

Goblin Slayer nodded. "I said I would ask what I needed to for the quest report."

§

As boisterous as the cheers from the crowd were, here, they felt dreadfully far away. Here being a tunnel leading to the field of battle, under the spectator seating. This was a place only those who were not yet winners—but were not yet losers, either—could go. It was isolated from the sunlight, illumination provided by just a few candles.

It almost looks like a dungeon, Priestess thought and then chuckled to herself.

She herself had been in a dungeon proper only once or twice. Nonetheless, the sense of prebattle tension in this place was very much the same as what one felt in an underground labyrinth.

She stood there among the echoes of the shouts above, which came in like waves on the shore. A racer covered in honor, her svelte, beautiful body clothed in colorful garments. A single shooting star flew across her forehead: Silver Blaze.

She stood with her eyes closed, appearing distant, as she waited for her great race, but it certainly didn't mean she wasn't ready. She was like a bow before it was fitted with an arrow, taut as a string.

Thus Priestess, the only other one left there, hesitated greatly to speak to her but finally said, "I'm sorry… I wasn't sure if before or after the race would be better. But I couldn't help thinking… I really felt I ought to talk to you."

"Yes… Of course." Silver Blaze blinked several times, drawing her gaze away from the nothingness. "It's fine. Probably better before I run. Yes, definitely better."

Priestess thought she understood what Silver Blaze meant, more or less.

"I—"

"I've been thinking about a lot of things," Priestess said, cutting off the centaur, hoping she had understood correctly.

Silver Blaze didn't respond but made a gesture that might have been one of amusement or her way of saying she wasn't interested. Priestess didn't mind either way. She hadn't been looking for an answer anyway.

"In any case…"

He'd said the kidnapping by the coachman and Silver Blaze's

disappearance had turned out to be unconnected, and she was sure it was true. If the coachman had tried to sell Silver Blaze with an eye to profit, the whole thing wouldn't have blown up the way it had. Silver Blaze would have surely reappeared at some arena or another, her silver lock hidden with hair dye or something. There was also the possibility that the coachman could have killed Silver Blaze when the matter began to get out of hand.

"But since you're standing here, he obviously didn't." Priestess tapped a thoughtful finger to her lips.

That, however, still left one question: Was it the immortal sorcerer who had killed the lanista? Or was it the doing of some passing goblins who had seen the pretty centaur girl and murdered her escort without a second thought?

If he was killed by goblins, though…

Then Priestess wouldn't have expected the body to be left in an identifiable state. Because he was a man? Hardly. Priestess remembered the awful death of that warrior she knew so well. It was simply the way of goblins to enjoy tormenting their prey, hurting them.

Whether goblins or sorcerer, the corpse wouldn't have been left as undisturbed as it was.

All right. All right. So if it wasn't the sorcerer, and it wasn't the goblins, and it wasn't the coachman…

"There was only one other person there with that lanista," Priestess said.

"…"

Silver Blaze didn't respond right away but looked at her feet, checking them like an adventurer about to burst into a dungeon chamber. And then she let out a breath gently, something close to a sigh of resignation.

"One of my friends has bad hooves, but she never lets on," she said. "She always runs with all her might. With a sound like lightning."

"Ah," Priestess said, remembering. The lovely centaur racer from the other day's race, whom they'd met at the *ludus*.

When she saw Priestess's expression, Silver Blaze nodded briefly. "She has tremendous power in her legs but also a large body. Her hooves can't take the strain."

"Well—"

"But it doesn't stop her from running."

There were many other racers, too. Those who ran flat out, vying for the win. Those who simply loved nothing more than running. Those who were totally committed with a consuming desire for victory. Silver Blaze spoke of them one by one, spoke of all those against whom she had raced. She looked the way Priestess did when she thought of friends past and present.

Thus it was, Silver Blaze told her—thus it was that…

"Thinking of them, I finally couldn't stand the idea of letting a race go to nothing just for some bets."

That's probably the whole truth of that night.

Even Priestess, somewhat naive about the world, could understand, more or less. Someone desperate for money had sought to cut Silver Blaze's legs in an attempt to manipulate the race's outcome. You only had to observe the furor when she had gone missing, and the passion on display now, to understand: The legs of this beautiful centaur, forged into tools for the sole purpose of running, were worth their weight in gold.

Silver Blaze looked at Priestess and understood that all had been communicated. The smile she gave the young woman then was almost translucent—it was a fleeting wish and the knowledge that that wish would never come true.

"So… What are you going to do?" she asked.

"Me? Nothing, really," Priestess answered without hesitation.

The centaur's eyes widened. Her ears, which had been standing straight up, flicked, and her tail swished. The body language could not have been clearer: She didn't understand what Priestess meant.

Priestess shook her head slowly and puffed out her modest chest proudly. "I'm an adventurer who came here to rescue a centaur princess and exterminate some goblins."

All else was speculation, without proof. Whatever might have happened between Silver Blaze and some lanista with a debt to pay off, Priestess didn't know. Perhaps that detective they'd supposedly summoned to the city wouldn't have let the matter lie, but she saw no need to pursue it.

An interrogation in the name of the Supreme God using the Sense Lie miracle might have found criminal wrongdoing. But—ah, yes. Priestess felt it was wrong to have to carry that weight. To have something like that weighing you down as you tried to run.

"You're Silver Blaze. That young woman's princess and this arena's…racer." It was Priestess's mission to protect, heal, and save. Including this beautiful woman who had been born to run. For *her* mission was…

"Therefore, I believe you ought to run."

"……"

Just as Priestess had chosen to walk the path of an adventurer, Silver Blaze had chosen to come here, had made it here, in order to run.

There was a very long silence from Silver Blaze, who took a deep breath in, filling her chest, and then let it out again. Then with her four feet, she stamped on the ground, a sound of resolution.

"Very well," she said. "I'll continue to run. Will that be good enough?"

Of course. Priestess nodded. *Yes*, she thought, *that will be good.*

Silver Blaze's expression was no longer pellucid; now a fire burned in her eyes. She was going to wage the contest of a lifetime with her companions, those who ran with her. So Priestess prayed for Silver Blaze, prayed for her victory, the centaur who stood there facing away from Priestess, looking gallantly toward the racetrack.

Then she said, "Oh!" It sounded so silly.

Silver Blaze, caught by surprise, scuffed with her hooves again, then stopped. She turned, and there was confusion on her face. "Is there something else?"

"Oh, no… Um…" Priestess blushed furiously, and she tried desperately to think of what to say. Argh, this wasn't getting her anywhere. But it would be pointless if she didn't press on.

She was distinctly embarrassed, distinctly hesitant, but nonetheless she managed to look Silver Blaze in the eye and said, "D-do you suppose I could have one of your horseshoes…?"

Silver Blaze blinked her beautiful eyes, then smiled. "Yes, I think so. I'll make sure to put my very best luck into it." Then Silver Blaze began walking, like a fresh breeze, out into the sun-soaked arena.

©Noboru Kanna

Priestess let out a long breath as she watched her go, then spun on her heel and set off at a quick trot. After all, she wanted to get back to the spectator seats just as quickly as she could. She couldn't miss this.

She was urged along by the cheer that came from the audience somewhere above and behind her, the sound of a crowd welcoming a hero.

§

"Well, that sure sounds like it was a pain in the ass!" Spearman said with a not-particularly-sympathetic chortle.

"Believe me, brother, it was," Heavy Warrior groaned, resting his chin on his elbow.

They were at the Dear Friend's Ax, and the tavern was busy and bustling, just like it was every night. Maybe even more than usual. If nothing else, the centaur waitress, one of the stars of the establishment, was wearing a particularly lovely smile this evening. Her hoofbeats sounded light on the floor, and each time she passed Heavy Warrior's table, she shot him a meaningful look.

Spearman watched Heavy Warrior wave back at her, and his grin got even broader—and a little meaner. "Hey, you *sure* it was a misunderstanding?"

"Shaddup. Who do you think I am, *you*?"

"Oh, it ain't a misunderstanding with me."

Heavy Warrior settled his chin back on his fist, wondering why Spearman seemed to think that was something to be proud of.

But I'm afraid if I open that door, a carrion eater might come out.

Adventurers might delve into dragons' dens, but there was courting danger and then there was courting *danger.* And besides…

A young lady is happy, and what's better than that?

The uproar that the centaur girl Baturu had caused had been a bit of a headache, but in the end, it had helped this situation get resolved. Because of it, adventure had been born into the Four-Cornered World.

"You know what they say: '*The gods knoweth adventure, and wot that it is without end. Though the great run of them threaten not the world at large.*'"

"Well! Someone's been hitting the books."

"I've been studying my brains out the last few days. Not even any adventures."

Heavy Warrior was the picture of a man to whom Female Knight had been putting the screws. Needless to say, Spearman found it quite a gratifying accompaniment to his drink. He had just come back from an adventure himself, and the beer couldn't have tasted better. Well, maybe it could have if Witch and Guild Girl had been there, but that wasn't to cast aspersions on a couple of men sharing a good drink together.

There was, however, one thing that might have bothered him.

"Where's our guy?" Spearman asked, tearing off a bit of smoked meat with his fingers and stuffing it in his mouth. It was cooked perfectly. "I saw the centaur girl around, so he must be back, too, yeah?"

"He's right where he always is." Heavy Warrior grabbed some salt with his fingers and sprinkled it over potatoes that had been cooked in oil. Oil and salt always made a delicious combination. "He made his report and scurried on home."

"Bah. Where's the camaraderie?"

"You know it's how he works." Heavy Warrior chuckled, then held up a hand to summon a server.

"Coming!" came a voice accompanied by nimble hoofbeats.

"The going rate is one drink," eh? Pfah! Heavy Warrior thought, privately resolving to grab the guy by his metal lapels and drag him out here someday.

"Ah, well. I can just imagine the kind of stories he'd tell," Spearman said with a shrug as he ordered another beer. "Goblins."

"And nothing but!"

§

"There were goblins."

"Oh, I see."

"They were riding on dogs."

"Ah, you mean wargs. And how many were there?"

"An entire tribe, perhaps."

"Was there anything else? I mean, besides goblins."

"A good question."

"..."

"There was a sorcerer."

Goblin Slayer finished his report, still unsure what was so amusing.

This was Guild Girl he was dealing with. Her pen sped across the lambskin paper even more quickly and easily than usual. She didn't even seem to notice the way her colleague in the next seat was looking at her with open amazement.

As for Goblin Slayer, he piled on the words relentlessly, calmly, as he always did.

Nonetheless, it wasn't exactly a complicated situation. Silver Blaze, the centaur princess, had gone to the water town to become a racer. On the edge of town, she had been attacked by goblins. He had simply pursued and slain them, and rescued Silver Blaze in the process.

As far as he was concerned, that was the entirety of the present incident.

"I'm certainly glad it turned out the way it did," Guild Girl said with a smile.

Yes. Goblin Slayer nodded very seriously at her. "I'm happy that the girl they kidnapped was safe."

"That's not what I'm talking about," Guild Girl said. No, not that. She neatened her papers pointedly, cleared her throat, and continued. "What I'm pleased about is... Well, I know you're still hunting goblins all the time...

"...but you seem to be having fun."

The meaning of the words was somewhat opaque to Goblin Slayer. Even as he left the Adventurers Guild, the door swinging behind him, and walked out into the twilit street, he didn't really understand.

Fun?

Who? Well, him, of course.

Guild Girl seemed to be smiling especially brightly about something—and that, he felt, was a good thing.

The road back to the farm was always so long and always so short.

Somehow it was never far enough for his dull wits to get his thoughts quite together.

"Oh! Welcome home!"

So it was that, somewhat sooner than he would have liked, he found *her* offering her usual greeting. Maybe she was in the process of getting the cows back in the barn, or maybe she was just finished. The young woman who spent all day at sweat-inducing labor showed no sign of the fatigue, there in the evening, but only smiled at him.

She greeted him with a broad wave, to which Goblin Slayer responded with a nod. "Yes. I'm back."

She jogged up to the fence, and they walked along on either side of it, as they always did. The evening was rapidly descending, the twilight shadows slipping away into night. But something was different from usual.

"Hup! Oops..." Something inspired Cow Girl to hop up onto the fence. However, she wasn't a child anymore, and it wobbled unsteadily under her weight. Quicker than he could reach out a hand to steady her, she regained her balance. "Used to be so easy, huh?" she said with a giggle.

She scratched her cheek with some embarrassment. Then she started off, hopping from fence post to fence post as if on stepping stones. He walked beside her, looking up at her, seemingly so far above him.

It's all things I don't understand.

Even things he thought had made sense to him as a child, things he had been able to do—now he could not manage them at all. People were supposed to grow and change, but how much growing or changing had he actually done?

"So? Did your adventure go well?"

"Yes."

"The...princess, was it? The centaur one? Was she all right?"

"Yes."

"Then I'm glad."

"Is that so?"

"Sure is!"

"I see."

Cow Girl waved her arms and legs like a clown as she worked her way along the fence. Abruptly, Goblin Slayer remembered the weight in his item pouch. Well, he hadn't exactly forgotten, but he had been having trouble judging when would be the best time to give it to her.

I would know what to do with a goblin: seize the initiative and make the first attack.

Gods, but this was so difficult.

"Huh?" she said as she meandered along. She looked perplexed. "Do you hear something rattling?"

"Hmm…"

He stopped and thought, then riffled through his bag as Cow Girl watched him from overhead. He came up with a plain, simple horseshoe, shining a dull silver. He held it out to her, and Cow Girl took it, blinking, then stared fixedly at it. She flipped it over, and on the back, she found engraved, in flowing, lovely characters, a name she didn't recognize—Silver Blaze—and a recent date.

There was one thing she definitely did understand about the object: that it was a souvenir he had brought her, and that it conveyed his feelings.

"This is one very fine horseshoe!" she said.

"It'll keep away bad luck."

"Well, thank you!"

When they got home, she would have to hang it over the door.

No sooner had she promised herself this than she glanced over—and found he was gone. She looked back to discover him halted once more in the deepening dark. She could sense his eyes were focused on her from under the helmet, watching her reaction.

"Tell me," he started, almost in a murmur. "Did it sound like it was fun?"

"For who?"

"For me."

Cow Girl didn't answer immediately but took a small hop to the next fence post. She wasn't as good at keeping her balance as she had been when she was a child.

I guess because I've grown up, she thought.

She found the thought a little embarrassing and a little disappointing—but there were traces of happiness in it, too.

She flapped her arms a little, letting her body do what it needed to keep its balance. She answered his question with a question of her own: "Did you have fun?"

"I'm…," he said, "not entirely sure."

"Okay, well… Hup!" Just as she was about to lose her balance completely, she somehow managed to jump onto the fence board itself. "Was there anything that made you think, *That's good*?"

"Hrm…," Goblin Slayer grunted softly.

When he thought back on it, in fact, there were several.

Encountering the red dragon in the desert, for instance. Or the fact that the dungeon exploration contest had gone so well despite all the commotion. The fact that he had been able to visit the northern seas. And one time he had even rescued a centaur princess.

And too…

"In my party," he said, his tongue still stumbling over the word, "there's a cleric of the Earth Mother."

"Uh-huh! The girl, right?"

"Mm." The cheap-looking metal helmet nodded, the tattered tassel fluttering in the evening breeze. "She's done a lot of growing. I think she's become a fine adventurer."

He didn't add aloud: *Not like me.*

He was Goblin Slayer, yes—but the girl, the young woman, she was far ahead of him as an adventurer. As she had shown on this recent quest.

"Does that…," Cow Girl began, hopping across another two or three fence posts, her red hair bouncing and swinging, "make you feel lonely?"

"Don't be ridiculous," Goblin Slayer said with a laugh. Yes: He laughed, a sound like a rusty hinge. "It's a very good thing."

And then he took another step forward.

AFTERWORD

Hullo, Kumo Kagyu here! Did you enjoy *Goblin Slayer* Volume 15?

In this story, goblins appeared on the open plain, so Goblin Slayer had to slay them.

I put my all into writing it, so I hope you had fun!

There are several recurring ideas and images in this volume, be it *ave, Caesar!* the "horse" races, or Sherlock Holmes. And at the heart of it all is "Leave it to the adventurers!"

This book is the closest I've come to doing a straight "tabletop RPG replay."

The kidnapped centaur princess and the adventurers who venture hither and yon to bring her home. The tribal strife, the squads of assassins, the romantic rivals, etcetera, etcetera. This is no heroic saga but a down and dirty tale of adventure, of a kind I first learned about via the *Sorcery!* books. It was tabletop RPGs, however, that showed me the pleasure of a group going along, chatting and bantering, screwing things up, but nonetheless pressing on. It might not involve the fate of the world, it might not even earn you much in the end, but it's nonetheless an adventure.

I've made it through countless adventures in the past, and I always think they're good things. Well, okay, so sometimes you wind up in multidimensional space or dying in all the 3,000 worlds at once, but still…

In any case, there's no end of adventures in the Four-Cornered World! This is just one of them.

I'm happy to say that a supplement has been released for the Goblin Slayer TRPG. It's thrilling to know that my readers are able to enjoy the Four-Cornered World for themselves.

On that note, this is another book that could have come together only with the help of many different people. Everyone in editorial, Kannatuki handling the illustrations, Kurose doing the manga, and all those in the distribution network. Not to mention my friends and everyone who picked up this book.

Thank you all so much.

In the next book, goblins will appear in the royal capital, so Goblin Slayer will have to go slay them! It'll rock you!

There's lots of other *Goblin Slayer* stuff going on, too, including a second season of the anime. I'm working hard to make sure things keep getting to you in a timely manner, so I hope you enjoy everything that's out there. See you next time!